PETTY TREASONS

VICTORIA GODDARD

PETTY TREASONS

For Alexandra Rowland, with thanks

THE NEW SECRETARY

I t was a beautiful space, the official study of the Last Emperor of Astandalas.

You—the Last Emperor, the Lord of Rising Stars, the Sun-on-Earth, the god—paced the long room. Fifteen strides up, twenty-five down, ten back to your desk. Your yellow robes swished pleasantly against your legs. Heavy silk; Imperial Yellow in colour. A dye compounded of ingredients from five worlds, used only for the person of the Emperor himself.

Yourself.

(Myself.)

Perfume wafted around you, faint notes of roses and ambergris and that cedar-like unguent from extreme eastern Voonra whose name you always forgot. In your mouth the air was cool, sweet, like water.

The walls were made of polished kyrian alabaster, chosen to be as free from inclusions or admixtures of colour as possible. Each white panel was carved very shallowly with a tracery of vines that took every faintest hint of

another colour and transformed them into deliberate lines,
refusing to admit even the hint of a shadow, a flaw.

The walls cradled the early morning light tenderly, the
translucent stone glowing. Back when you yourself had
glowed, faintly shining even in your most ordinary
moments, the walls had glimmered in the corners of your
eyes, white and gold upon white and gold, so refulgent it
was hard to see the corners of the room.

There were windows, deep-set in embrasures that were
screened with more carved alabaster, under eaves that
prevented any direct sunlight from entering, even when the
sun was very low in the winter sky, back when this palace
had been in temperate Astandalas the Golden, not equatorial Solaara.

(Such a strange and terrible mystery, that translation of
a building and its inhabitants—*one* building and its inhabitants—from one world to another, when the magic that
bound an empire of five worlds together crumbled and fell.
You—*I*—did not understand what had happened; nobody
did.)

Your path traced the spaces between the windows and
doors: fifteen strides up, to the table at the top of the room
on which stood a jewelled mechanical nightingale in a
golden cage; twenty-five down, to the doors set with ivory
and ebony panels that led deeper into the Imperial Apartments; ten back up, to the desk made of intricately carved
sandalwood from southern Voonra.

You brushed our hand lightly across the edge of the
desk, silken-smooth golden wood, aromatic, barely a sensation on your fingertips.

Two windows on the outer wall, either side of the
nightingale. If you stopped a few paces back, at the point
where you could just see the spear of the lefthand guard in

the corner of your eye, you could see through the alabaster tracery.

There was not much of a view given the angle of the Emperor's Tower and the fine disregard of the architect to any possible desire to look *out*. In Astandalas you had been able to see a fragmented wedge of the city, smoke rising up over tiled roofs. Sometimes there had been pigeons, and in the winter great billowing murmurations of starlings.

Here the windows faced northeast, and you could see the line of a river meandering to the sea that stretched out across the horizon. White birds wheeled past: gulls and terns and egrets, and sometimes, sometimes, there would be a flight of multicoloured parrots rising up from the gardens or pink flamingos returning to the salt pans in the south.

One of the guards shifted his weight from one foot to the other, the butt of his spear scraping quietly across the floor, some metal item about his person clinking. Otherwise there was no sound but the snap of your sandals on the floor as you started to pace again, the swish of your robes about your legs, the waiting for the next bell to sound.

Up fifteen strides, down twenty-five, ten back to your desk. You kept your hands loosely clasped behind your back and your face serene, your shoulders down. Perhaps you might change out the art on the long eastern wall, you mused, pausing with your back to the outer door.

The left half of the wall was exterior, gently luminous in the morning light, but the righthand side had rooms behind it, and the wall was opaque by comparison. One of the chambers was accessed through the next room in of the inner apartments; the other had a door to this one. That had been a service room once, before you became emperor, kept hidden behind a vast canvas painted with the pornography your uncle the previous emperor had … favoured.

(It was art, the best of it, for all that all of it was porno-graphic, and even though the genre hadn't in itself entirely bothered me—albeit I knew I—*you*—you the new Emperor, plucked out of exile to take the throne—you were *expected* to find it strange—some of the subjects were disturbingly *young.* Nothing I had found out about the previous emperor endeared him to me.)

When you had come to the throne, unexpectedly and to no one's satisfaction, all of the art had been burned in a parody of the ceremonies of purification. You had had them scour all the rooms in the Apartments to the bare stone.

There was no privacy in the life of an emperor. Appar-ently your uncle had found that, or learned to find that, titillating.

You paced.

Up fifteen strides, down twenty-five, ten back to your desk. The current pictures were ones you had chosen in those first, bewildering months after being crowned Emperor. Five paintings of landscapes, one from each of the five worlds under the rule of Astandalas, empty of people and serene of effect.

The one from Zunidh was outdated, depicting as it did the classical heartland of the Empire, Kavanor of the first cities. From the reports most of the continent of Kavanduru had fallen into the ocean, and Kavanor was nothing more than a few remnant islands and a turbulent new sea.

(Northern Dair had been covered by lava flows, and half of what had been the Northern Ocean was a boiling expanse of near-volcanoes. There was a wall of storms across the Wide Seas, a chain of typhoons and hurricanes and cyclones drifting from one sea to the next. Very little had been reported from Southern Dair past the near edge of the Erchilingian jungle.)

You did not know what had happened to the rolling hills of the Geir in the northern Vale of Astandalas on Ysthar; or to the fantastic forests of giant bamboo on southern Voonra; or to the Sea of Pinnacles on Colhélhé; or to Orio Bay and the island of Nên Corovel on Alinor.

The passages between the worlds of the Empire, so straightforward, even mundane, under the magic of Astandalas, were now hazardous ventures indeed. There had been a few reports of people lost in the Borderlands who had stumbled out on Zunidh, but their stories had been nightmarish and unclear.

What could you put in place of these landscapes of lost realms?

(Lost responsibilities, no longer mine to worry over, to govern or to judge or to ruin.)

There had been a tapestry, you recalled, tribute from Colhélhé. A hand-woven chart of the the full extent of the Empire at its height, beautiful and accurate without being too detailed. Accurate enough, even now, you suspected. A reminder.

You turned towards the empty desk your new secretary would be using, as soon as the next candidate arrived. You could set him that task, couldn't you? To go wrangle with the Treasurer to find the tapestry map?

Yes. If you remembered correctly the map should extend most of the length of the wall. It would add a certain warmth to the austere room, without marring the general effect.

It was a beautiful room, you considered, if perhaps a trifle empty. Things had broken during the Fall which had not yet been replaced. There had been a fine sculpture of a chained lion on a marble plinth, there, tribute from a conquered city, memento — not exactly *mori*. Perhaps it had been meant as a reminder that the wheel of fortune turned even for emperors.

The sculpture had made of your pacing triangle a rhombus. Or perhaps it was a trapezoid?

(I had never cared all that much for geometry; but I did, had always, would always, care about using the correct word.)

The chained lion had been a trifle too apt, you reflected, turning again at your desk, glancing up at the one moment you could see the sea through the windows, lowering your gaze to the floor as you swept past your guards, gripping your hands together behind your back, just for a moment, when only your face was to them.

The new secretary was not actually late.

You paced, aware at a level simmering just below conscious thought that it was ten minutes to the ringing of the hour-bell and the coming of the next candidate.

Your guards stood at precise, unvarying, perfect attention. There was not much room for the expression of personality, standing at precise, perfect, unvarying attention for six hours at a time. You did try to learn their names; you had not had any occasion to say them outside of accepting their oaths of service. You did not have even that for any of your other attendants.

Sergei, the senior, was on the right; Ludvic, the junior, on the left.

You were the single most important person in the Nine Worlds. You had learned not to ask too much of those around you. For one thing, it was never taken as *asking*: even your most carefully casual comment was taken as an implicit order. You had learned to keep your thoughts to yourself after a wistful comment about cherry blossoms had ended up with the College of Wizards rearranging the entire magic and most of the climatological system of Ysthar to provide a new season in the Vale of Astandalas.

Now that you were the Lord Magus of Zunidh, and no longer technically Emperor of Astandalas (*no longer* because Astandalas had fallen in a great and terrible cataclysm; only *technically* because the subjects of the remaining portion of the empire refused to accept this demotion), no one could do such a wholesale work of magic besides you.

They could still interpret your comments as the next thing to a new decree.

And to be honest—not that you had much opportunity to be honest—the Fall of Astandalas had largely put paid to such great works of magic. You struggled more than you had let anyone see with wrestling the broken and distorted magic of Zunidh. You had wrought no magic, all that time as Emperor, and though your magic had awoken with you after the Fall, it was still … unruly.

The College of Wizards had crowned you Lord Magus, when the previous lady had thrust the role onto you in panicked relief, but no one really thought you could do more than the barest minimum with respect to the magic. It burned that you had not yet been able to prove them wrong, that all you could do was be the centre around which the rest turned.

Up fifteen strides, down twenty-five, ten back to your desk.

It was better, proper, *courteous* to keep your thoughts to yourself, and your expectations for companionship low.

You did insist your chief attendants not be wholly and unbearably obsequious. This had proven a much more diffi-cult thing to achieve than you had ever countenanced.

In the three years—or so; one of the problems concomi-

tant on the Fall was the bizarre and nearly incomprehen-
sible disarray of time—since you had awoken from the
coma induced by the Fall, you had gone through seven
grooms of the chamber and well over a dozen personal
secretaries.

You were beginning to fear you would have to settle for
impenetrable formality as the best you could hope for, the
wall of thorns around the sleeping, silent castle. A barri-
cade, at once protection and barrier.

When you were Emperor the taboos had been iron
bands around you. They had delineated everything about
your life, from what moment you were awakened through
to when you were finally able to close the bed-curtains and
for seven blissful hours not be seen by anyone but yourself.

You had not been able to avoid seeing yourself, when
you were Emperor, for the magic inherent in the position
had made you glow. It had been bright enough to read by,
when you were unable to sleep.

You had had to create a soft mage-light, the first few
months after you had woken after the Fall, so accustomed
had you finally become to the ever-present illumination. (It
had been at once a triumph, for the magic worked, and a
shattering grief, for I—you—I—needed it.) Your guards
had said nothing, though they had called attendants to
check on you, the first time you had endeavoured to go to
sleep without the light. They had feared for your life, when
the light went out. You could not blame them for that. All
the lights had gone out when Astandalas Fell.

After that they seemed to have taken the old Imperial
fiction of the divinity of the Emperors and made it into
literal, worshipped, fact. Even your attendants; even your
guards. They saw you in every room, every state, every
moment, except for those precious few minutes each day in

your private study, those hours behind the curtains on your bed; and perhaps that was enough, for them to take you as divine.

(I had always been good at showing people what they wanted to see.)

Up fifteen strides, down twenty-five, ten back to your desk. You stopped to regard the outer wall again, the faint tracery of carvings on the luminous stone. Outside the sun was climbing high, no longer reflected on the sea. You had not been outside for … two months, was it?

You had lost count. That was a good thing, you supposed. You had kept an obsessive count of all the hours it had been since you became Emperor.

(Fourteen years, four months, four days, seventeen hours, and then the Fall.)

There was a soft knock on the outer door. You did not turn while one of the guards answered and spoke to the guards on the other side. It was five minutes to the hour, the third hour since dawn, nine of the old clock: your guards changed at dawn and noon and dusk and midnight, precisely six hours apart here on the Equator. This was not that, and so therefore it was the new secretary-candidate.

One of the guards (the righthand guard, Sergei, from the direction of the sound) thumped the butt of his spear down on the floor in the quiet, easily-ignored indication that someone who was expected had arrived.

It was up to you, of course, to condescend to greet whoever it was.

You flicked your hand to indicate they might open the door to the new secretary.

You stared at the wall, the painting of the plains of Kavanor, the hilltop cities, for a moment longer. And where were they now, those ancient cities lost to Yr the

Conqueror, first Emperor of Astandalas and your ancestor after nearly one hundred generations? Audar, Essur, Kithor, Zard. All gone, razed by ancient armies, their ruins fallen into the sea.

You could hear the new secretary breathing; his breath came faster than the guards at parade rest. No doubt the man (woman?) was nervous. You had dismissed the last candidate halfway through his obeisances for the miasma of pure blind terror the man had projected from an untrained magical gift.

This candidate had no gift of magic, trained or otherwise. You traced out the taste of magic in the air, straining against the heavy weight of wizardry here in the heart of the Palace, the former heart of the Empire, still the heart of Zunidh.

The new secretary was from far away—still of Zunidh, but there was a glimpse of—what was it?

A night scene: a small, unfamiliar boat, a man—two men?—upon it, sails catching starlit wind, the doubled prow plunging through black waters and brilliant phosphorescence, the sea to the horizon, the stars above bright and clear and *familiar*, pearls floating down the River of Stars, the spaces between as luminous as the waves—

A gift of a moment, a place far away, a hint of friendship and adventure … Nothing for you, but for the briefest scent of salt as the vision faded.

You blinked back the hint of tears before you turned.

Not that anyone would be looking at your face, but even so. Even so.

The door was closed, and the new secretary-candidate stood framed by the two guards.

Next to their perfect physiognomy and height, he was decidedly ordinary. Average. He was dressed in the uniform of the Imperial Bureaucratic Service with no indicators of rank outside his status as a, yes, Fifth-Level Secretary. The pale grey-brown linen did no favours to anyone's colouring.

"Cliopher sayo Mdang, Glorious One," Ludvic announced. His Azilinti accent made the *a* in *ang* sound out long and sharp. *Mi-ðaaang*.

Sayo? This was the first time the Master of Offices had sent anyone not of noble rank as a secretary, which suggested that either the Service was even more thinly staffed than you had thought, or that this unassuming man was extraordinary. Or perhaps both.

(Eventually, eventually, even the Master of Offices would have to admit defeat in the silent contest they were playing and send someone who was reasonable. It was a numbers game, and you — I — had learned patience.)

You regarded the man thoughtfully, assessing, not letting your gaze linger too long, climb too high. One sweep up and then down again, careful not to meet his eyes, which were lowered according to the custom.

Custom. Taboo. It was skirting perilously near for you even to glance up at the man's face from across the room. The official pronouncement was that seven ells was safe. Seven ells: over twenty-six feet. You should really be standing up by the jewelled nightingale, if you wanted to look anyone near the door in the face.

Cliopher sayo Mdang was about the same age as Ludvic the guard, a decade or so younger than yourself: probably still in his thirties, even early thirties. He had golden-brown skin, broad shoulders, and silky black hair cut short in the style used by the Service. He was perhaps more fit than the usual run of secretaries, if the drape of his robes was any indication. He was clearly nervous, by the faint tremble in his hands, but performed the obeisance with only minor hesitation.

He had practiced, that was clear.

The secretary did not know any of the discreet gestures you used, and so for the first time that morning since you had finished the morning ceremonies, you spoke out loud. Your voice resonated through the room, the acoustics catching it into something musical despite the neutral intonation. "Rise and take your seat."

Cliopher sayo Mdang was more awkward rising from his prostration, but that was common enough. He was also visibly relieved to be sent to the secretary's desk. Well, perhaps he'd heard of the candidate dismissed before he'd even finished the obeisance.

The bells rang the hour. Cliopher sayo Mdang took the opportunity to set out his pens, brushes, inks—including a traditional inkstone, which was interesting—and an array of papers. He was finished and attentive before the bells had finished tolling.

Two points before you'd even started. That was enough to win him the position, to be honest.

The Glorious One—such an absurd array of titles you possessed! Some days you felt most at home piling them up upon yourself, a child building cloud-castles, a poet spinning fancies, a fool trying on names—decided not to question your new secretary, for fear of what you might learn, and instead launched into dictation. Your new secretary was responsive and polite and thoroughly, *gloriously* focused on the work before him.

One quarter-bell, two, three. Cliopher sayo Mdang wrote quickly, neatly, easily, his brush singing across the pages before him. His hands were sinewy and strong, deft in his craft but surely shaped by other skills. He asked no questions other than the odd request for clarification, and those were few and far between.

Three points, four ... Could this be an *actually* competent secretary at last?

Surely not. The Master of Offices had never attained so high. Sometimes you felt, you the Last Emperor, you the Lord Magus of Zunidh, you the Lord (still, somehow) of Five Thousand Lands and Ten Thousand Titles, you felt that the Master of Offices was just that bit worried what might happen if his ostensible lord and god took a greater hand in the running of the government.

Instead you were given all the broken magic to mend, which they did not think you could do (and which I could not do, though I tried; I tried), and the glory of being the figurehead, and the honour of being the still, stable, central point in the dance of society, and that was surely enough. More than enough. Even in these trying times, what luxury was not yours to command?

(Up fifteen strides, down twenty-five, ten back to my —*your*—the desk. Don't ask such questions.)

Just before the midmorning break, when the household attendants would bring in refreshments, you turned to dictating a series of points about the various regions of the world insofar as they had been reported. It was dispiritingly full of war and the rumours of war. Not to mention all the natural and magical disasters. Except for, where was it? Yes —the Vonyabe—

"I beg your pardon, Glorious and Illustrious One?" said your new secretary.

Glorious *and* Illustrious? You considered the secretary, whose head was bent down to his desk. He was bravely endeavouring not to show his anxiety. His voice was a low tenor, pleasant on the ear, the sharp rural vowels a refreshing change from the lilting court accent.

You wondered what the man's singing voice was like, before corralling your thoughts back to the matter at hand.

"The Vonyabe," you said, slowly. "It is in the former Imperial Province of the Wide Seas."

Sayo Mdang hesitated, very carefully not looking up. And then he said, his voice nearly, nearly calm, "Ah, yes, the Vangavaye-ve." His voice lingered on the sounds, savouring the vowels, briefly musical. He wrote the name down with a swift flourish, no hesitation over the spelling.

It had been —

You stopped. Glorious, Illustrious, Radiant, Serene —*Most* Serene, even—it had been a very long time since anyone had corrected you.

An hour and a half since Cliopher sayo Mdang had arrived.

You regarded your secretary with narrowed eyes, intent suddenly on winkling the man's character out of him. The man sat there, shoulders back, spine straight, eyes on his paper. His right hand holding the brush nearly steady; a few droplets of ink were beading on its camel-hair tip, catching the light in winking flashes.

Yes, *indeed*. Cliopher sayo Mdang knew *exactly* what he'd just done.

You had always endeavoured to be precise with words. Use the correct one, in all instances. Rejoice in learning something new. "The Vángavaye-ve, then," you said, mimicking the pronunciation, and continued with the rest of the sentence and a return to your steady pacing.

As you turned away from your secretary's desk, you caught the younger man's faint exhale of relief and, with your own back to the guards, permitted yourself a small, fleeting smile.

～

To *competent* and *intrepid* you had to add—oh, what a delight it was to have to do so!—you had to add *unrefined* to the adjectives you might bestow upon your new secretary.

Oh, Cliopher sayo Mdang was not discourteous; not in the least.

Or—the pun was too great—he *was* discourteous, but only because his manners were polished for far different company, under far different principles. There was very little of the courtly about him. His accent was defiantly rural (where? The Von—*Ván*gavaye-ve? Surely only someone from there would care enough about its pronunciation to interrupt the Sun-in-Earth in order to correct it!); and though all the key behaviours were performed assiduously, they were endearingly, obviously, *performed*.

When the refreshments came in, you the Lord of Rising Stars moved another piece in the game you were playing with your secretary, and offered him some.

Your secretary might or might not have realized you were playing, but instead of making either of the obvious moves—either to accept or protest the offer with fulsome compliments—he said, "Thank you, my lord," and continued on with his notes.

A very few minutes later Sayo Mdang realized his mistake; but instead of producing some overabundance of courtly manners to recover, he merely bit his lip and continued on as he had.

It was a delight. Competent, intrepid, unrefined—what *else*?

~

He had a sense of humour.

No one had a sense of humour, not around the Wearer

of the Crown of Living Flame of Zallahyr. (Not even though the Crown of Living Flame, which I'd once found, had turned out to be a disappointingly mundane item made of electrum and fire opals set on little dangly wires. I'd left it in its spot in the Treasury, in a pile of ancient gems that could probably have ransomed three kings and their consorts. Occasionally it showed up in the rotation of jewels, reminder of a splendid half-hour sifting through the flotsam and jetsam of history with no one else close to hand.)

At the end of the morning, you and he had managed to get through more work than the three previous secretaries had done in their entire combined tenures.

Admittedly, that was only three weeks and two days: three weeks for the third-last, two days for the second-last, and nothing at all for the most recent, but even so. Even so.

You wondered if you dared, and found you did. Cliopher sayo Mdang was packing up his writing materials, waiting for the last page of notes to finish drying before he made his obeisances and departed to wherever it was Fifth-Degree Secretaries went when they were not taking dictation.

(I had a brief, amusing vision of all the secretaries trundling back to their rooms, one after another, and tucking themselves comfortably next to their writing cases on a shelf, ready for the next day. I—you—had to hold court tonight, for those aristocrats who remained rattling around the Palace. I could imagine the quiet, unassuming pleasure of being tucked away for the next day, no one to call me out of myself if I wanted them not to.)

You waited a moment, until the younger man was half-distracted, and slid into the air a line.

It was a good line: perfectly innocuous by itself—or, at

least, mostly; even here, even now, you were (I was) who
you were—and yet also an opportunity.

Your new secretary caught the innuendo, and not only
that, threw it back, with a razor-sharp twist that delighted
you so much you replied in kind, in turn, in joy and secret
awe and—

And Cliopher sayo Mdang laughed out loud and looked
you straight in the eyes as he declared it a perfect riposte.

I stared at the younger man, shocked.

(*I* did.)

Cliopher sayo Mdang had dark brown eyes, sharply,
brilliantly alive, full of merriment fading into horror.

You tore your gaze away, snapped back into your imperial self, benevolent and serene and all that folly of a
pretence of divine equanimity. Your new secretary fell
rather than descended into his obeisance, eyes glimmering
with welling tears. At your automatic dismissal Sayo
Mdang turned and fled, writing kit forgotten on his desk
and magic reverberating in the air.

The door snicked gently into place, the two guards
standing at their precise, perfect, unvarying attention.
Sergei on the right, Ludvic on the left. Sergei from the
former duchy of Kolascz on Ysthar before the Fall, Ludvic
from Woodlark in the Azilint of Zunidh.

They did not meet your eyes; they were far too well-
trained for that.

You took a few moments to compose yourself before
you could say, quietly and calmly: "Send after Sayo Mdang
to return his kit." You gestured at the leather box. Your
guards would be looking at your hands, to ensure they
missed none of your unspoken orders.

You, even you, even after everything, had to take
another deliberate breath before you could say the next
sentence. "If the taboo against looking full upon our eyes

holds, see that he has all the medical and other assistance he needs. If ... if it does not, inform the Master of Offices that we are pleased with his choice and duly appoint Sayo Mdang as our personal secretary."

"Very good, my lord," said Ludvic, saluting.

Ludvic never let anything rock him. He had been the safe harbour in the storm after the Fall. One day he would be promoted to something more than just one of your personal guards. One day.

You (yes—*you*—the Protector of the People, you the Shield of the Empire, you the Sun-on Earth) turned and went into your private study, where no one, not even the guards, not even your servants, not even *the Emperor* went.

You stared blindly at the dim room, lit only by the one square of brightness high up on the wall, the only unscreened window in the Imperial Apartments.

You sank down on the bench immediately inside the door and briefly, just briefly, buried your face in your hands as you thought how pleased you had been (*I had been*), a quarter-hour before, working with the man you might have just permanently blinded.

You held court, Glorious and Illustrious and Most Serene, in stiff robes of gold-embroidered white samite over gold ahalo cloth. You wore the Lesser Gauds, for it was one of the many small holy-days of the court. Possibly it was your official birthday.

You sat on your golden throne, on the dais fifteen feet above eye level. The jewels were heavy: yellow diamonds and golden pearls in simple chains, layer upon layer across your shoulders, around your throat, around your wrists and your ankles, your waist and your forehead. Gold leaf had been painted on your eyelids by your attendants. As always you had kept your eyes closed the whole time they were attending you.

They had seen your face at close quarters, but you had never seen theirs.

The golden pearls and the ahalo silk came from the Von —the Vángavaye-ve. You savoured the sound of the name in your mind, your eyes on the patterns of the dancers below. The floor of the Throne Room was another map of the five worlds of the Empire, jewels set in silver. The courtiers wore slippers, soft-soled, to protect the precious stones. You could not quite determine where the Vangavaye-ve began in the expanse of lapis lazuli that delineated the Wide Seas of Zunidh.

Your attendants had lacquered your nails with gold, fingers and toes. They had slipped rings on your fingers, your toes, gold set with diamonds, with pearls, with citrine and topaz and every glittering yellow and white jewel. They had anointed you with more perfume, roses from Ysthar, kvalin from Colhélhé, musk from Voonra. Every time you shifted position slightly a little burst of scent filled your nose and your mouth, as if you were eating rose petals, drowning in amber.

You had not walked down to the throne room. There had been the gilded litter, borne by six of the guards, with six more ahead of you, six behind. They had made a solemn procession down the winding ramp that spiralled around the core of the Palace, from the heights of the Imperial Apartments to the Throne Room on the ground floor. It was a way for those who could not attend the court still to see you, to be reassured that you were alive, that you were awake, that you were sane, that you were there.

It was not true you never looked upon anyone's face. The throne was fifteen feet above the floor, and the lower dais swept out far enough that anyone on the main floor was at least the requisite seven ells' distant. You could recognize your courtiers by their faces as well as their gaits, their shoulders, their hands, their garments, their voices. They looked upon you, always, one eye watching you, taking in your appearance and bearing as indications of the state of the world.

You sat there on the golden throne, the golden cushion, in your robes of gold and white, breathing in the perfumed air that held still and serene around you, perfectly still and perfectly serene, watching your court dance.

The music was good, of course.

The first hours of the day passed as they always did. The sunrise ceremonies, abbreviated as they were compared to what they had been in the Empire, still took time. You prayed for your people, to the real gods above you, and took the time to try to settle your magic.

Even now, three years after you had woken from the coma after the Fall, three years after your magic had come cringing back to you, like a beaten dog wondering how much more pain it would take to be forgiven, it was still raw and painful, still tender and tentative, still passive and remote.

All those years as Emperor had affected it, you knew, and the Fall as well. A hundred years comatose and three years recovered—

If that *hundred years* and those *three years* were true. That was what the priest-wizards said, and you perforce had to believe them. It was not as if you would know if no one told you directly. The guards did not gossip in front of you, or even to you; no doubt the rumours of your early behaviour as Emperor still lingered.

(I was sure there had been more than three official birthdays, even if when I pressed my memory I could not imagine why I thought so, for though the hours, days, months, years seemed endless, they always seemed endless. Fourteen years, four months, four days, and seventeen hours; and then the Fall; and now the future unspooled before me, uncertain, entirely changed, and yet entirely the same.)

You prayed, and attempted to settle your magic, and bathed, swimming vigorously in the pool for a good half of an hour. You would have stayed in the water longer if you'd dared, relishing the feel of it on your skin, the fact that you could duck your head below the surface and, for as long as you could hold your breath, be alone and yet embraced in warm welcome.

You could not hold your breath long, though each morning you tried to go a few strokes further.

You prayed, and attempted to settle your magic, and bathed, and were dried off and dressed by your attendants. Black today, and gold-figured black above. Only your signet ring on your fingers, no rings on your toes. A belt of onyx set in gold worked into the shape of ivy leaves, tiger's-eye agates round berries between the links. You closed your eyes as one of your attendants used a sponge to rub lotion into your bald head, then even more gently, more carefully, across your face.

You broke your fast on flatbreads and bittersweet marmalade, the closest you could come to fresh fruit, and tea. You read the morning's reports, wondering whose neat hand had scribed them, whose quick wit had summarized them, whose anonymous brilliance was thus displayed. It was not whoever had been doing it the week before.

Your guards stood at the door that led into your official study, their eyes on the wall behind you, one facing to the left of you, one to the right.

Your magic darted around the room, tasting the magic around Ludvic and Sergei, still on the morning duty. Sergei's magic was twisted around itself, seeking a home that no longer existed. Ludvic was much more restful, settled in himself, the connection to Woodlark comfortable and secure.

There. A quarter to the third hour of the morning, nine of the old clock, sonorous here as it was everywhere in the Palace except the Throne Room. In there one could hear only the great bell that rang the four quarters of each day, entirely unintimidated by petty human concerns. Not that anyone who spent more than a few days in the Palace did not come to be excruciatingly aware of the rhythm of the bells.

You rose, and strode towards the door Sergei had immediately opened. The guards looked out; from the corner of your eyes you could see their heads turned, as if for threats; as if there would be any threats, here in the innermost chambers of the Imperial Apartments, that did not come from you.

You went into the study, preparing yourself for what you knew was going to come. Yet another secretary, no doubt nowhere near so competent, so intrepid, so unpolished, so funny.

You would have to ensure that Cliopher sayo Mdang had all that he needed. Healing. *Mind* healing, after so abruptly losing his position, his profession, his sight. A way home. If he were from the Vángavaye-ve, entirely the other side of the world, would he want to go home?

(What had brought him here in the first place? Through all those wars and rumours of war, those natural and magical disasters, that *wall of storms* across the Wide Seas? Why had he come here, to the Palace, to become a Fifth-Degree Secretary? What had he left behind? What had he hoped to find? What dreams were now ashes in his hands? Had he lost everything in the Fall, and come to the Palace in the hopes of making some future for himself?)

You paced up the long room, ten strides to your desk, fifteen to the jewelled nightingale in its golden cage, twenty-five down. Ten back up, and there you paused, looking back across the room at the wall along from the guards, where the first state portrait of yourself as Emperor hung.

Artorin Damara, hundredth and last Emperor of Astandalas.

It was recognizably the face you saw in the mirror when you bothered to look, if younger and less serene and more handsome. One might almost catch a hint of personality in the quirk of the lips, had there been any emotion in the eyes. Those were painted flat gold, neither whites nor irises separated, as the convention had it. No pupils there to let in the light; not when you were ritually and ceremonially, legally and by custom, magically pinned and bound there at the centre of the Empire, its ostensible sun.

Fourteen years, four months, four days, and seventeen hours, and then the Fall.

One hundred years, the rumours said, comatose, laid out on a bier on the lower dais. You (I, I, I) had wandered in dark dreams until something woke you, and three of the four guards at the corners of your bier startled and panicked and faltered from their posts.

All except Ludvic Omo, standing steady as a rock on the lefthand side, who let nothing rock him.

Three years attempting to make some sense of the world left to you, the broken government and devastated lands, the unpeopled countries and the tender, tentative, tattered magic.

On your desk were the piles of reports you had been reading over breakfast, duplicated with some convenient spell the wizards of the Empire had long since perfected and kept largely to themselves. You knocked the edge of one pile just slightly out of square, your hand like a shadow. When you had been Emperor you had cast no shadow. Black of skin, but radiant, gleaming, glowing.

A faint, quiet knock, and Ludvic tapped the butt of his spear on the floor.

You closed your eyes, just for a moment, and gestured for them to open the door. You could face this; you must.

And yet, Cliopher sayo Mdang was there.

The man was subdued and even more excruciatingly polite. He looked wan, exhausted as if he too had slept little, and his hands trembled more than the day before as he set up his desk. There would, it was clear, be no jokes this morning.

But he was there.

The relief was extraordinary: like a gush of cool water falling upon your head, drenching you from head to toe until your eyes swam with rainbows. You whirled around, away from the secretary, the guards, the door to the outer world, your painted imperial self, and busied yourself frowning at the outdated landscapes on the wall, the plain door that led to your private retreat.

The bells tolled the third hour, nine of the old clock, the beginning of the session. You took three long, quiet breaths in, even more gently out, and blinked your eyes sharply against the rainbows. The alabaster wall was even more luminous than usual, no doubt catching some resonance from your magic.

The last note died away, and you turned not directly to your new secretary, to Cliopher sayo Mdang—to Cliopher, you would name him so in your mind, to Cliopher who had given you the greatest gift you had received in all those years of tithes and tributes since you became Emperor—but began to pace.

Up fifteen strides, down twenty-five, ten back to your desk.

"Good morning," you said, not fidgeting, not looking quite in your secretary's direction. "We are pleased to see you today, Sayo Mdang."

Cliopher replied with something you might have taken as genuine fawning, had you not had the previous day's behaviour to consider. And also—for although you *appreciated* the man's restraint, it was notable—the display of fawning gratitude persisted barely more than half an hour, and even that seemed to be nearly beyond Cliopher Mdang's willingness or capacity to play the game of courts. At one point he even flicked his glance up to see how you were taking it.

Your eyes did not meet, for yours had slid off the man's face a bare instant before, automatically lifting away as you came near, but you caught the motion in the corner of your vision as you turned at the bottom of your triangle.

Up fifteen strides, down twenty five, ten back to your desk. Each time you turned away from your guards, your new secretary, you smiled, and you looked at the flat golden eyes of your state portrait with something akin to compassion, for even if the future stretched on uncertain, there was this unexpected benison for *you*, who supposedly provided all your people needed.

A look, a word, a smile, a metaphorical hand outstretched across the ocean moating you —

You received the tiny, inconsequential offerings Cliopher Mdang gave you with disproportionate joy, a child opening birthday presents.

Inconsequential was not perhaps the right word.

You didn't dare search for the right one. Not yet.

SMALL MIRACLES

It was a week, a month, a year, of small miracles.

It was hard to tell time, to grasp hold of anything but the bells, the round of ceremonies, the glittering evening courts. Some nights you dreamed of your courts, that you were caught in some faerie enchantment, metamorphosized entirely into gold, that you were become in truth the idol you were created.

For the weeks, months, years, since you had woken from his coma you had been unable (or was it unwilling?) to enter into time. There were strange reports from outside the Palace: stories that in one village it had been a handful of years since the Fall, and in its neighbouring village across the river, through the forest, on the other side of the mountain, it had been a handful of generations, even centuries.

(I believed the reports.)

Every time you turned around it was another stage of the performance. You closed your eyes so the gold leaf might be applied. You opened them, and it was court. You laid your head upon the silken cushions, the downy mattress, closing your eyes on the carved wooden canopy, the opulent curtains. You rose, and bathed, and dressed, and performed your ceremonies.

You wrestled with magic. Your own magic, the world's magic, the tattered and torn remnants of the Empire; all of it whirling uncertainly, broken and battered, tender and tentative.

You opened your mouth and spoke the ritual blessings. You closed your mouth and ran your hand along the edge of your desk, moved the papers just slightly out of alignment. You paced, fifteen paces up, twenty-five paces down, ten back to your desk. You spoke decrees, wrestled a simulacrum of good government out of the general anarchy, the threadbare bureaucracy, the skeleton army, the surviving nobility, the starveling populace.

They all wanted order, stability, a central point on which to rest their hopes and their minds: you could be the last, at least; at the very least, to the very last. You could be the idol to whom they prayed, knowing the gods had not heard their cries when the Empire and all its magics came tumbling down.

Your household had been decimated like all the rest in the Fall, in that hundred years comatose. (How? Why? How could it be that there were men and women around me who remembered my coming to the throne, as I remembered myself coming to the throne; remembered before then, when I had not been even a name to the courts, to my own family: I the second heir of the Empire, the back up, the spare.) You knew their names, the soft hush of their voices, their hands never touching you, ghosting around your skin with brushes and dressing wands and gloves.

And then. And then.

Enter Cliopher sayo Mdang.

Add that one competent, intrepid, unpolished (*funny*)

secretary into the even, enchanted tenor of your days, and the kaleidoscope began to—

Not shift. It shifted all the time, shuffling those same elements into their infinite permutations, each recombination subtly different from the one before, fascinating until the essential sameness cloyed.

Add Cliopher sayo Mdang into the mix, one speck in that ugly brownish-grey uniform that suited nobody, a pebble amongst all the yellow diamonds and white alabaster and jet, and the kaleidoscope slowly ... stopped.

Those first few days, that first week, that first month, it was just—you told yourself it was just—that you were concerned about any lingering consequences to that accidental meeting of gazes.

Each morning, at five minutes to the third hour, nine of the old clock, you were there, waiting in your official study for the door to open on your secretary, leather box under one arm and the neat, undistinguished, plain Fifth Degree robes.

You greeted him, each morning the same words, so that at first you did not realize the spinning was slowing, would soon stop.

"Good morning, Sayo Mdang."

And, in a tiny, unbelievable gift, treason according to the absolute letter of the law, Cliopher sayo Mdang would look up after his obeisance and *meet my eyes* and smile and say, "Good morning, my lord."

One moment each morning in which you spoke as a person to another person, and was greeted as a person by another person: on such did the entire machinery of apotheosis stutter to a halt.

~

You became increasingly suspicious that Cliopher sayo Mdang was smarter than you were.

At first it seemed a simple matter that Cliopher was clearly much better at anything to do with numbers. *You* had never liked them; had never found anything about mathematics appealing. You did not like the mathematics of magic used by the Schooled wizards of the Empire. You did not like geometry or algebra for their own sakes, and the entire concept of fluxions was something you were grateful to have forgotten.

Cliopher had a positive relish for budgets. It was uncanny.

He was also disconcertingly efficient. You requested him to find the tapestry map, which he did: it was hanging on the wall by the next morning. When he entered that day, Cliopher also presented you with an accounting of the current state of the Treasury, which had surely been in some of the many reports you had read over the days, weeks, months, years before he came, but to which you had not paid more than the slightest necessary heed.

No *less* than the necessary heed; you had your pride, distant and risible as it seemed to think you might. But the numbers washed out of your mind as the kaleidoscope turned, never any better, sometimes worse.

You paced up fifteen strides, twenty-five down, ten back to your desk.

Cliopher mentioned that the Treasurer might respond well to a personal audience.

You considered your responsibilities, and eventually agreed.

With the new tapestry map in place there seemed to be a lacking object on the other side of the room. You remembered the marble plinth that had once held the chained lion, and how you might find another treasure that you admired out of those your ancestors had looted.

One day, therefore, you did not spend your afternoon wrestling with impossibilities, with unbound magic and hungry spirits, with time that ran like water or puddled like honey. Instead you called for the litter and descended the spiral to the level below the Throne Room, where the Treasury honeycombed the Palace roots.

The tithes and tribute and plunder of a hundred Emperors was gathered there. After speaking with the Treasurer, words falling out of your mind, your mouth, you walked through the rooms, magic lighting your way though the Treasurer and her staff had brought torches. Five thousand lands and ten thousand titles. So much blood. So much gold.

In one of the storerooms was a vase, asymmetrically glazed with teal.

"This," you said, remembering the flash of a kingfisher's wing, on a river far from the Palace, once upon a time.

With the vase on a new plinth, your route shifted.

Ten paces from the inner door to your desk: the scent of sandalwood, the silky-smooth wood, the papers, the serene countenance of your own portrait a reminder of who you were and what you were not. Fifteen strides up to the jewelled nightingale; that infinitesimal pause to glance out the window at the moment you could see through the alabaster screen.

Ten strides down to the ebony plinth.

Fifteen strides to the door.

No.

You had them move the ebony plinth, but you did not

like that either. Twelve strides down; thirteen strides down; no.

You paused in your pacing, frowning at the plinth.

"My lord?" said your secretary, after a long silence.

You had forgotten entirely what you were dictating. You turned, lifting your eyes to meet the other man's quizzical smile.

Some atrophied sense of the absurd made itself known in your heart. After due consideration, you permitted yourself to ask, "What is the difference between a rhombus and a trapezoid, Sayo Mdang?"

Sayo Mdang blinked, once, twice, his eyes bright and intrigued. "A rhombus has all of its sides parallel but its angles acute, my lord," he said. "A diamond, for instance. A trapezoid has two sides only in parallel. In some places such is called a trapezium."

In another mood, in another life, you might have made some quip about trapeze artists. In this mood, in this life, you frowned at the plinth, at the shape your route took. "And if the sides are all of them out of synchrony?"

"In that case it is a quadrilateral, my lord."

"A shape, that is, with four sides."

"Indeed, my lord."

Maths. Bah.

You turned back to your desk, ten strides up, scent of sandalwood, and glanced across at the ebony plinth and then at the guards on the door.

Ludvic was still, or again, on morning duty, and when your glance crossed his face, the guard met your eyes calmly, his expression warm. He had brown eyes, darker than Cliopher's, more widely set in a broader face.

A slight hitch of your own breath, hands clenched painfully behind your back, and then you said—serene as if this was not the second person, the second gift—you said, "Guard Omo, will you move the plinth back another foot?"

Ludvic saluted, leaned his spear against the wall, and moved first the superlative teal vase to sit on Cliopher's desk, where the secretary could regard it with cautious, concerned awe, and secondly moved the plinth, and thirdly returned the vase to its spot before he returned to his.

Up fifteen strides, down twenty-five, ten back to your desk. But now when you strode past the middle of the long wall, your footfalls set up a very soft sympathetic chime from the vase.

"A triangle is a more pleasing figure," you said to no one in particular.

"Indeed, my lord," said your secretary, head bent, voice threaded through with amusement.

You remembered that you were speaking about the pirates reported off the coast of southeastern Exiaputl, and continued on.

Slowly, incrementally, things changed.

Cliopher sayo Mdang continued to offer his small gifts, his petty treasons, each of them casually, as if he did not realize he was even offering them. As if he did not realize he was humming the banned, brilliant epic *Aurora* as he finished an official declaration, brush singing across his paper, while you paced up fifteen, down twenty-five, ten back to your desk, slow and steady, hands behind your back, face more serene than the painted portrait, giving no indication whatsoever that either of you knew the infamous poem.

You might have believed his innocence, had you not had

come to realize just how brilliant a mind worked behind that unassuming exterior.

Up fifteen, down twenty-five (the soft chiming ring from the glorious kingfisher-blue vase, the colour of a moment long ago but cherished, polished in my heart as if it were the only stone in my treasury), back up ten to your desk.

Cliopher finished that particular proclamation just as the fourth hour of the morning tolled. He stopped humming and instead busied himself cleaning his brush of the gold-flecked black ink he had been using. By the time the fourth toll fell away into silence he was ready with his pen and a clean sheet of paper, face nearly calm, eyes brimming with unspoken mirth.

Surely Cliopher had to know what he was doing?

Offering these gifts, moments of transgressing social norms—moments of transgressing *laws*, though it was not quite a crime to hum that song; only to sing or speak or read or write or print its words—moments of him being a real person, as if *you* were a real person, too.

(I would not see the humour if I did not look upon the man's face. I would not know it was there if I were not also stepping over those norms, reaching out past those taboos, looking back. But there had never been anyone to cross over for, before.)

How long had it been since Cliopher had come to you? Already you could not quite recall what it had been before, when you had been sleepwalking, when you had been caught in the enchanted moment of the transition from the mortal to the divine. A soap bubble, glistening, brilliant, floating on air, caught on the end of a child's wand, held trembling there. Popped in a gush of relief.

The old myths of metamorphosis were full of rape and transgression: violence was done to those who crossed between those realms, who were torn from the human and made divine. To be drawn back —

"And have you decided what will you be working on next, my lord?"

You blinked, realizing you had been speaking, dictating something. Cliopher's page was half-filled with the arcane symbols the scribes used. You could read them, had learned them in your other life, before you had been given the crown and the sceptre and the throne, but upside-down and several strides away you could see only that there was something about storms.

You could not recall what you had been thinking. "Read out the last few lines," you ordered, spinning around and returning to your desk. Why did you even have a desk? You never sat at it. *You* did not need to write anything down, not with Cliopher sayo Mdang there, his neat hand singing across the papers; nor look anything up, not with Cliopher sayo Mdang of the prodigious memory and sly humour.

You used it in the afternoons, sometimes, when you were doodling a mimicry of magical formulae.

Cliopher read out a few lines and you remembered you had been intending to clarify what exactly the last few reports from the coast had said.

"There continues to be strange weather along the eastern coastline, then," you said, turning to look at the portion of the woven tapestry that dealt with eastern Dair. It was not in the centre; the old Astandalas had been placed in the centre; and so Zunidh was to one side. You found the tiny jet bead that marked Solaara, then a village notable only for being the childhood home of Yr the Conqueror and location of the Imperial Necropolis.

A silver thread marked the river, green cross-hatching the infamous Solamen Fens. The coast meandered mostly due south, greens and browns on the landward side, blue and aquamarine for the Eastern Ocean. Silver marked the mouth of the Orcholon and the islands of the Azilint off the coast. You tapped your fingers on the copper threads depicting Woodlark, Ludvic Omo's island. The threads were soft under your hands, warm under your fingertips, tiny gemstones pinpricks of sensation.

You *touched* so little.

You could not bear to test that taboo. You had burned a woman nearly to death, when you first became Emperor. You had swung around when she came too quickly up to you in your peripheral vision, unaccustomed as of yet to omnipresent servants, and your hand coming up in instinctive protection had touched her wrist.

You could still hear her muffled screams, the stench of burning flesh, the horror that that taboo had bound you with its power. What if it still held? You could not pick someone to test it on to see.

"Indeed, my lord, there have been a recurrent series of severe thunderstorms along the coast, with concurrent waterspouts."

You forced your thoughts back to the topic at hand. You noted the mild pun of con*current* waterspouts, but made no response. After a moment Cliopher continued.

"The villages along the coast and somewhat inland have been reporting rains of fish and other bizarre phenomena."

You considered that. "What kinds of fish?"

What kind of question was that? What did it matter to *you* what kinds of fish were falling out of the sky onto the bewildered inhabitants of the coastal villages? Why would Cliopher Mdang even know?

But he did know, because of course he did. He was a *competent* secretary, after all.

"Rains of fish generally happen when a waterspout or

windshear crosses a shoal of forage fish—that is, small schooling fish that gather in large numbers near the surface, like malago, rockfish, pilchards, or sardines. They are heavily predated, and there have been reports that some of the larger predatory fish species have also been seen inland."

Somewhere in the back of your mind was a memory of seeing one of the great fish migrations running along a coastline: miles of fish a grey current in the water, bombarded by gannets and gulls, seals and whales and sharks and thousands of other fish cutting through the shoals, fishermen in gaily painted boats hauling in nets full of wriggling, writhing silver. The water boiling like a pot on the fire, the sky full of splashing and skreeling birds.

"Are the fish alive when they fall?" you asked, a note of curiosity entering unbidden into your voice.

"Often," Cliopher replied. "The present storms are particularly vicious, and the waterspouts they spawn larger and more numerous than usual. There are reports coming from a hundred miles inland of the fish."

You paced up to the jewelled nightingale, down to gaze pensively on the teal vase. "Does it ease the famine?"

It was an easy guess there was famine. Everywhere there was the tumultuous and confused weather, the breakdown of trading systems, the flares of magic, the strange hiccoughs and variations of temporal order.

You wore silk and ahalo cloth and finest muslin, gold and jewels and rich, strange perfumes, all of them out of the vast hoards your ancestors had gathered into the storerooms of the Palace. No new tithes had come in, only the necessary supplies of food and raw materials. Your household was still working through the spices and rare ingredients kept for your table, but you doubted the rest of the Palace was so fortunate.

"Such fish need to be salted immediately," Cliopher replied. "There has not been enough dry weather for salt production to be at its usual height in the saltworks along the coast south of Port Izhathi, and the city requires a great deal as well. The great salt flats of Northern Dair were destroyed by lava, and of course, trade farther afield continues to be … intermittent."

"Have we no stores in the Palace?"

Surely you had ordered them kept, when you were Emperor. Surely you had taken thought for a possible emergency.

(In Astandalas the Golden the priest-wizards had bound the very weather to their magic. There had been no crop failures in the Vale of Astandalas. Outside the Vale the part of Ysthar that was *not the Empire* was an arctic wasteland, miles-high walls of ice crushing continents, dry winds blowing sand and snow across endless steppes, all the magic siphoned for the glory of the Emperors. I might not have remembered to think about emergencies. But the government had not been entirely incompetent, back then, even if it did not have Cliopher sayo Mdang in it.)

Cliopher made a note, a sharp tick with his pen, the nib catching on the paper. "The priest-wizards have tonnes, my lord, but they will not release them. They say they require it all for their ceremonies and rituals. It is purified, they say, far beyond the requirements of salting food."

So. So. Cliopher sayo Mdang had views, did he, on the priest-wizards and their ceremonies?

Come to that, so did you. So did I.

"We will speak to the Ouranatha," you said, returning to your pacing, falling into the easy stride, the rhythm of your mornings. "A rain of fish ought to be a blessing, not a curse."

It was not as if the Ouranatha were holding the magic of five worlds in their net; not any longer.

Up fifteen strides, down twenty-five, ten back to your desk. "What other phenomena are they experiencing?"

Fifteen waterspouts seen at one time, a record. Rains of squid. Pure white crocodiles swimming up the Orcholon. Giant watergoing thunder lizards. Snow.

No doubt at some point you would receive something made of the white crocodile skins, a tithe-offering to the local god.

"There was an account recently, my lord, of a giant waterspout. The disk was a good two hundred feet across, so the report says, before the winds whirled up ..."

Cliopher's voice continued, describing the scene. You thought of a waterspout you had once seen forming, too close for comfort (but oh, so greatly exhilarating, so magnificent, so *grand*. I had not always been *comfortable*, nor wanted to be.). The dark disk skating across the water, catching the eye with its discrepancy.

The water spraying up, magic spiralling up, like a djinni forming out of the sand in a legend, a broad base for the narrow wavering column of water vapour that reached up from sea to sky, staggering drunkenly across the wind-whipped sea, a one-legged giant.

"It cut across the waters between two of the Azilinti islands, churning the water. The sardine run had moved south by then, but there are places there where the mako-pare—that is, a kind of hammerhead shark—gather in great numbers."

"Are sharks not solitary?"

"Indeed, so are most species, my lord, but the mako-pare, the hammerheads, are known to form schools, sometimes many hundred strong. Off the Azilint is one such gathering-place."

You imagined them. Had you ever seen an actual hammerhead shark? You didn't think so; had only seen pictures. They were often depicted in stylized form in coastal Jilkanese art, in the carvings of some of the Azilinti islanders, probably in arts of the Wide Seas Islanders as well. You could picture the surreal, alien heads, the eyes at each end of the hammer.

"The waterspout crossed the school, and was of sufficient size and strength that the surface winds picked up the makopare and bore them across the the Viurgyr Channel and up the mouth of the Orcholon towards Dinezi."

Dinezi was the largest community in that region, a sleepy provincial capital known primarily for having a splendidly carved palace frontage. It was quite far upriver because of the crocodile swamps at the mouth of the river; higher up, there were plains and far fewer mosquitoes before the jungles began in the mountain foothills. After the Fall it had collapsed into squabbling factions, ripe with violence. Ludvic Omo had said that when he last returned from visiting his village on Woodlark he had been told not to enter the city for fear of his life.

(I had not always remembered to ask no questions. In those first exhilarating, terrifying moments between discovering my empire had fallen and being handed the new government by Lady Jivane, I had been free to ask questions, and receive answers. Ludvic had told me almost more in that half hour than I had learned since.)

"The city was holding a competition to determine the next leader. They have an ancient contest where they chase elephants through a certain canyon near the city. They paint the elephants with indigo and henna, tie ribbons to the elephants' tusks, and whoever is able to collect the most ribbons without being gored or trampled is considered the victor."

"A dangerous game," you observed, noting its parallels with other forms of establishing social dominance.

"The contestants are unarmed," Cliopher said blandly. "In this instance, the elephants had been driven into the mouth of the gorge and the race had begun, with the elephants stampeding downhill and the contestants waiting along the route. They jump from large boulders onto the elephants, if they can."

You pictured it. The elephants—large-eared, long-tusked, enormous—their grey hides decorated with blue and umber, trumpeting and thundering down the canyon … Would the stone be red in that region, red as the Escarpment north of Solaara?

Say yellow. Yellow sandstone, the painted elephants festooned with ribbons, white and yellow and red and blue and green, surely, flashing and snapping in the sunlight, the wind of their motion. The young men and women leaping from the outcroppings and boulders, their skin a darker red-brown, their wild wiry hair bedecked with flowers, their lithe arms painted with the same henna and indigo as the elephants.

The air would be hot, electric with excitement. No doubt all the locals crowded the top of the canyon, looking down at the fools wanting power and acclaim, laughing and cheering and jeering and shouting their encouragement. The air would be heavy with the musk of the elephants, the dust an acrid dryness in the mouth, washed away by the sweet corn-beer they made down in that region, the fiery golden liquor made from the heart of palms.

There would be bonfires, meat sizzling on the coals, soft floppy breads to soak up the juices, the rasp of charcoal, the dashes of hot-pepper sauce to wake up the tongue. There would be fruit, watermelons in piles, red and pink and yellow flesh, sticky and sweet and cool, the flies buzzing round and the wasps.

I could taste it, see it, smell it, hear it, as if I stood there with the ground trembling underfoot from the weight of the elephants, the laughter in my ears, my veins, my own mouth, the golden liquor flung from hand to hand in a leather bag, the high flutes and the drums —

"Just as the elephants were reaching the lower mouth of the gorge," Cliopher said, "the waterspout crossed their path."

You opened your eyes.

You were standing by your desk, in the cool alabaster room, your hand on the smooth surface, sandalwood and jasmine and orange-flower neroli in your nose, your gaze on the prim and proper figure of Cliopher sayo Mdang at his desk.

Cliopher's face was nearly expressionless, but his eyes were bright, sparkling, challenging.

You kept your face court-serene, wondering what your eyes showed, to this single, solitary man who looked at them.

Cliopher folded first. "Everyone watched for the elephants to come down the gorge, the contestants running beside them or on their backs or picked up in the trunks of their own, if they were sensible and had trained with the animals in advance."

"A quality one might appreciate in one's new leader."

"Just so, my lord."

Cliopher sayo Mdang, it was clear, would be the sort of person who would ensure he trained with the elephants years before he ever planned to enter the contest.

More likely, he would be the person who assisted his chosen lord to train with the elephants. People did not stay Fifth-Degree Secretaries in the Imperial Bureaucratic

Service into their thirties if they had strong desires to sit on thrones. Stand behind them, quite possibly. Sit *on* them, very unlikely.

"No one was paying attention to the weather, save to note that there were storms to the east. The jungle and the gorge cliffs hid the ocean from view, and no one was looking at that direction. They were, thus, vastly surprised when the huge and terrible waterspout crossed the mouth of the gorge, hit the canyon walls, collapsed from its own weight and the sudden change in air pressure, and drenched the area with a considerable quantity of water and a hundred hammerhead sharks."

You looked at Cliopher sayo Mdang. Cliopher sayo Mdang looked at you.

There were many strange and bizarre occurrences in the world, even without taking into account the effects of the Fall. This was true.

It was quite possible for a waterspout to come sixty miles inland: this was also true.

There had been rains of fish and squid, some of them quite large, all along the coast; the reports were too many and too consistent to doubt it.

Cliopher sayo Mdang was trying valiantly to keep a straight face.

It could have been simply the inherent absurdity of the situation.

You narrowed your eyes, fighting suspicion. Little bubbles of incredulity were rising, popping against the back of your throat, tickling the back of your nose, making your heart snap and billow like a pennant on a windy day.

"The stampeding elephants skidded and stumbled on the mud and the fish, and several of them had to fight off biting sharks, for they were still alive—sharks can last a surprisingly long time out of water—and the contestants were forced to flee the scene, dropping their ribbons as they went. The elephants took the sharks to be their natural enemies, and turned on them, stamping and squealing with indignation."

The bubbles of mirth were growing, swelling, subsiding, rising up in little streamers of delight. (What was in my eyes, that Cliopher sayo Mdang's were so bright and merry?)

"Finally all that was left was one contestant sitting on the head of her own elephant. She held a white ribbon in one hand and a shark in the other, and no one could doubt that she was the true winner of the contest."

Cliopher's voice was nearly his usual delivery, save that his accent was sharper and more striking than his wont.

You held it in, the mirth and the delight, the sharp awareness of absurdity, the elephants and the waterspout and the sharks plunging down all unexpectedly upon them —

His secretary paused, and licked his lips, and then, carefully, cautiously, softly, his eyes still full on yours, the light catching them like sunlight in tea: "Digaourandé, they are calling her. The Shark Queen."

And — I could not help it — *I could not* — I laughed.

I lifted my hand to my face, hiding nothing, feeling your composure break and crack like ice dropped in water, the rolling laughs rising up from deep in my belly, exploding against my mind.

At last I — *you* — composed yourself. You looked away from the pleased smile on Cliopher sayo Mdang's face. Sergei was stiff and sober as always, his gaze trained firmly away from yours; yet you met Ludvic Omo's glance.

The second man, the second time.

Ludvic too was trying not to smile, his eyes warm and welcoming, his lips twitching.

You could not help but smile back, merriment subsiding into a quieter pleasure at this richness of gifts, before you turned around, paced back up to the desk, the jewelled nightingale, the windows.

~

Some few minutes later, serene once more, you said: "Surely that is not true?"

Cliopher looked down at his paper, a small, smug, self-satisfied smirk tugging at the corner of his mouth. "The following report does suggest that it was not one *hundred* sharks, but only forty, my lord. Though to be frank, if I may be so bold, even *one* hammerhead shark falling out of the sky would be quite the shock, don't you think?"

And *I* laughed again, because—because I could.

~

Your household must talk among themselves, for it was not long after you had looked at Ludvic (that I had laughed aloud, before others, for the first time in—so long) that you were standing in the dressing room, eyes closed, your attendants ghosting around him, the air thick with lilies and cinnamon, when one of them said, "Which parure would you prefer today, Glorious One?"

That was not a question you could answer with your eyes shut.

You knew the voice of the man, your most recent groom of the chamber. Light of step, nervy, slim, always dressed in the most exquisite clothing, hair shaved according to the aristocratic style. Accent the slight brogue of the northern aristocrats of the Vale of Astandalas on Ysthar before the Fall. His skin a light brown, his voice a light tenor, his commentary, to this point, negligible.

You did not decide your costumes. You could have; there was nothing stopping you from choosing. You might have informed your attendants that you would wear the one set of robes in Imperial Yellow, or the other, or the third; you might have said you would prefer white for the upper garments today instead of black; you might have stopped biting your tongue and begged for something red.

You opened your eyes.

Your groom of the chamber stood just before you and a little to the side, a tray held steadily in his hands. The tray was black lacquer, glistening like fresh paint. They were alone in the room, apart from the guards standing quietly behind you.

On a white silk square was the choker from the Dangora XIV Set: antique carved gold beads and black jet and the lustrous silver-black pearls from the Finturei archipelago of Colhélhé. On a black silk square beside it was part of the set that went with the Crown of Living Fire, delicate dangly wires and fire opals and all.

It could not be your official birthday again, surely. Even your actual birthday was far away on the other side of the year.

You glanced down at your garments. Black samite tunic. Ghostly-pale ahalo cloth two shades off from white in the direction of gold in the form of an open robe, the wide cuffs folded back to show the darker gold lining, all of it embroidered with tiny white seed pearls in the shape of suns-in-glory.

Black and white and gold (and Imperial Yellow) were the colours of Astandalas. The Sun-in-Glory was its primary symbol. Ordinary clothes, for the evening court wear of an Emperor.

The Crown of Living Fire did not go at all. The groom of his chamber (the Cavalier Conju enazo Argellian an Vilius) surely knew that.

When you had been Emperor in truth you had been intensely persnickety about your clothing and your jewels. There had been so little you could choose without consequence, for a period you had become somewhat tyrannical about what you could.

Naturally, there were and had been consequences to all your choices. Each ring and each necklace and each crown came with its own history and weight of significance. You had, for a brief period, relished that. It was that or scream; and you did not like to be considered mad.

After you had woken, after the Fall, you had, for a moment, thought yourself able to choose large things, though in truth they were no choices at all.

You *could* have walked away from the Palace, refused the mantles offered you, but out of the corners of your eyes you had seen the expressions on their faces. (All their faces; even Ludvic's, when he stood before you, before me, reporting on the state of things.) Heard how the bells had rung with triumph when the news spread that you had awoken at last. Felt the magic stir, testing the bonds that had held it in place; felt how thoroughly and catastrophically all the magic of the Empire had collapsed.

The decision not to leave your crown where it had fallen was the hardest decision you had ever made.

Once made, the walls and the taboos closed once more around you. Some few of them were relaxed; others were even more stringently to be obeyed.

You declared you would no longer be an Emperor, and so they made you a god.

There were places in the old Empire where the images of the gods were kept in secret recesses of temples, in intensely holy receptacles, except on particular sacred occasions. Then the images were anointed with perfumes and painted and gilded, dressed with fine garments and adorned with jewels. They were placed on bejewelled litters and borne in display, presented to the view of the faithful, who crowded close for a glimpse of divinity revealed through such mortal materials.

You had understood your role, once the immediate fog had cleared, and ... accepted it.

You had wondered sometimes if your attendants felt that they were dressing up a doll as much as you felt like a doll being dressed up. You had wondered what would happen if you declared the taboos broken.

(I had wondered what would happen if I stopped ... trying.)

You wrestled with magic, and attempted to govern the splintered remnants of your empire, and resigned yourself to being the golden figure holding still at the centre of the pattern, the linch-pin of the wheel if no longer the Linch-Pin of the Empire. You had tried not to let any one moment or one configuration dismay you, knowing all the same elements would be there in the next, and since you would not (I could not) leave them you must learn to live with them.

But now: enter Cliopher sayo Mdang, from the Vángavaye-ve or whatever far-flung hinterland region he hailed, and the spinning was slowing down, and the people of the household you had sleepwalked past for days, weeks, months, years had discovered you were waking up.

And therefore, this small choice of one set of jewels over another, a choice that was not really a choice—an easy choice, for someone long out of practice—was ... another small gift.

It didn't matter which of the parures you chose today,

except insofar as the fire opals did not go in the least with the costume you were already wearing, the person you currently were.

"The Zangora XIV Set, Cavalier an Vilius," you said presently, not stumbling over his name for all it was the first time it had ever crossed your lips.

The man's eyes widened and his hand gripped the lacquered tray tightly, just for a moment, before he continued on as if nothing had happened and nothing had changed.

The next morning, as if it had always been a part of the routine, you were offered a choice of two yellow robes: gently, easily, simply, as if you were coming out of a long, tiresome convalescence.

GREAT MAGICS

One morning (when? it was not long after Cliopher sayo Mdang came; not long after that conversation about salt; not long enough for the reports of waterspouts and rains of fish and the Shark Queen of Dinezi to have been folded into the muffling cotton of history), you made your ablutions and performed your prayers and tried to settle your magic, and your magic settled.

You sat there at your breakfast table, cup of tea in front of you, the air fragrant with a hint of blackcurrants and smoke. Your hands were loosely clasped around the porcelain cup, your eyes on the rising steam, posture excellent, feet firmly planted on the floor.

Everything the same as it always was, except that today, for the first time, your magic came to hand.

You explored it wonderingly.

That first morning as Emperor, you had reached out with your magic and found it redounding against all the bindings holding you at the centre of the Empire. A trickle of fire in your mind, a trickle of blood in your mouth. You had caught yourself before the fire and the blood could consume you, and pushed your magic *down*.

That first morning after you woke from the Fall, you had felt all the broken bindings and immediately reached for your magic. Oh, the *hope* you had felt, just for a moment—

Your magic had come, in fire and in blood, and so too had the broken world and shattered empire.

You had closed yours eyes and let the magic subside, no longer suppressed but certainly not *right*, and gradually, over the three years since, you had become able to do small tricks: call light and feel the origins of people and things. Passive, subtle, quiet things, no more than the small tricks of Schooled wizardry you had been able to do even as a boy.

There had been a morning, in your tower of exile, when you discovered your true gifts. All the world—all the Nine Worlds—all the *cosmos* at your feet, in that tower at the edge of the Empire, where the bindings were light and the Wild pressed close.

(There had been a book and a key in that tower of exile … I had left the book behind, but what had ever happened to that key? I had never found what it opened.)

Most wild mages could do next to nothing, and sometimes worse than nothing, with Schooled magic. You suspected your meagre abilities had mostly to do with your position.

As the Marwn, the second heir, the spare, you had been the unseen, unnamed, unknown counterpart to the Emperor in his glory. Astandalan magic worked in pairs and opposites, and if the Emperor were the obvious centre, the linchpin of the wheel of empire, the Marwn was the hidden bolt keeping the axle in place.

You had been exiled to the farthest edge of the Empire,

where its magic was thin. You had been able to learn wild magic, delving deep into the mysterious powers Astandalan wizards barely acknowledged existed. You had found the books left by previous scholars and mages in that tower, studied them, learned them, questioned them, made up your own spells and inventions.

And—

You stopped yourself quite consciously.

Those few people who might have thought to befriend the new Emperor had assumed you would have nothing to say of your exile as Marwn but for those few bare comments you did make that you had studied poetry and music and the philosophy of magic. And since you did not know quite what else you *could* say, really, about that decade and a half or so, which now (and even then, in those first months as Emperor) was as the memory of a dream, you had let them think that those studies had encompassed the whole of your life.

It was not untrue to say you had studied poetry and music and the philosophy of magic.

It would not be untrue to say you had studied wild magic and been forced to suppress it when you were crowned Emperor, because as Emperor you were the centre of all the Schooled magic. You embodied it in your actions, your words, your posture, your garments and your jewels and your gestures. There was no room, not then, for the magic that had once gallivanted freely as a far-flying bird.

(It was best to leave it at that, even in my own mind. That tower to which I had been exiled would hold my secrets as it had held many others' before me. I had not been able to work magic, and I refused to succumb to what came of *not working it*, and ... that was that.)

This morning, this morning, you settled into a light meditation on your tea, on the steam spiralling up, the calm, orderly magic in the room, the feel of Zunidh and the softer echoes of Ysthar and (softer yet) Voonra and Colhélhé and Alinor; and your magic was there.

You stretched underused faculties. The magic swirled, not simply passive perception and flinching reaction, but active, even eager, response to your will.

Not simply a call of light, practically every magic-user's first act, but a push out to the magic in the room and then in the Palace as a whole. Your mind traced out the lines of magic. The enchantments still binding you, those broken and those in effect and those in ill effect on you and those around you; out along the currents and ley-lines radiating out from the centre.

The land called you, the Palace gardens once of Ysthar, now of Zunidh. Or—trying to be of Zunidh. The magic had tried to knit itself together, but it remained strained and awkward, pockets no longer of Ysthar but not of Zunidh, traps and snares for the unwary and the unlucky.

The bells rang the third quarter. You noted how the sound anchored the magic, the notes pulsing through the intricate works of the Palace wizards and holding the whole together. Anything within earshot of the great bells that rang the four quarters of the day had come to Zunidh in the Fall, called home by some strange combination of magic and the desire of the bells themselves, which in the odd way of ancient objects knew their origin and their home.

You retreated from the trance but did not—could not—relinquish hold of your magic. Not this morning. Power swirled around you like your robes, crackled in the air about you, as you stood and strode through the ivory-and-ebony doors into your study.

You were a trifle late; Cliopher had already arrived.

"Good morning," you said.

"Good morning, my lord," replied your secretary,

smiling with a slightly apprehensive air no doubt due to the magic foaming in the room.

That precious morning exchange completed, you stood beside your desk, considering. Cliopher seemed to catch some inkling of your purpose on your face—even before you quite knew what purpose you might have—for the man hesitated over his pens and brushes.

You nodded acknowledgement, which he took as permission to question.

"Does your Radiancy propose another task this morning?"

That was ... not entirely ill-expressed. This morning you probably did seem His Radiancy, not glowing but with the air electric about you. And how to answer? You had not proposed 'another task' to yourself, but now that the possibility was raised—

A faint tremulous echo of the garden, the grounds, calling out in response to the bells decided you.

"Yes," you said briskly. "Prepare a report on the current activities and policies of the Ouranatha. We have magic to work in the grounds this morning."

"Very good, my lord," Cliopher replied, bowing, only a hint of surprise glittering in his eyes.

You swept out, Ludvic and Sergei (still? again?) falling into place behind, the magic tingling in your fingers, the soles of your feet, across the skin of your head.

You followed the call through halls you had never traversed and down a set of stairs you had not known existed. Courtiers and servants startled to see you, falling on their faces in shock, abject as if you were one of those wooden icons suddenly walking before them. You nodded regally, gesturing them to rise as you passed, to return to their tasks, not stopping (never stopping) though you could see their amazed, questioning, concerned faces in the corners of your vision.

And at last, suddenly, a door opened before you, and you were—*I was*—outside in the full sunlight of a tropical morning.

Equatorial, you corrected yourself. (You were still the Last Emperor, even here, even now.)

There was a gravel path under your feet, crunching under your sandals. The air was hot and tasted metallic for a moment before the wind rose and brought the scent of oranges to fill your senses.

For a moment you stood there, rocking your weight gently back and forth so the pieces of gravel squeaked across one another. The Palace was behind you, the world in front of you. And if you simply … kept walking?

Not simply. Never *simply*.

You were somewhere on the southeastern side of the Palace. You'd descended that mysterious staircase to the base of the Emperor's Tower, and was now in the gardens embraced by the long stone facades of the Zuni and Collian wings. One of the reports had said the Collian wing had been severely damaged by the Fall and that some ill magic prevented anyone from reconstructing it.

You had not thought it much of a priority, not with the Palace still at far less than half capacity. Out here in the gardens, Zunidh greeted you, magic whispering through the languid air across your skin, ruffling the diaphanous silk of your outermost layer of clothing (Imperial Yellow again this morning; from any distance you were unmistakably the Lord Emperor), warm under your feet even if wretchedly strained.

You had been an Emperor for those fourteen years, four months, four days, and seventeen hours. You had not perhaps been a great one, but you had done your best, and that was not so poor. You nevertheless had so little idea of what to do about the political unrest convulsing the world, the violence and anarchy, the collapse of government (the collapse of *your* government), the famines and the natural disasters and the wars—

The magic of the grounds, the gardens, swarmed up. It took visible form by catching up petals and leaves and insects, hundreds and thousands of them, swirled into skeins and unwound rovings of material.

For a moment they seemed near-natural, the wind gusting a somersaulting roll of fallen leaves, but then the wind darted forward to tug at your sleeves and hems and the leaves and flowers, the butterflies and bees, green and blue and white and yellow and purple and red, red, red, gathered around you, circled around you, skittered uncertainly between and behind your guards as if not quite sure whether they were part of you or not.

So. So.

(I might have next to no idea what to do about the rest of it, but this *I* could do.)

You took a breath, tasting the air, testing the magic. Fresh air, scented not with perfumes and unguents and oils, but by the world itself.

It was warm on your tongue, effervescent. The oranges retreated, leaving something peppery, a little sweet rot, just on the cusp of noxious. *That*, you thought, your magic responding to the thought, the crying, circling magic, the festoons of leaves and petals hanging like garlands in the air.

You followed the calling magic through gardens that blurred into green masses, the sun bright in your eyes and magic in your mind, for you certainly had no tears gathering in your eyes, no, not though you had simply walked out the door, down the gravel path, into the air, with no thought to the precautions and ceremonies the Ouranatha had declared so essential.

You were not even wearing a hat.

(The last time an anointed Emperor of Astandalas had walked in open sunlight without any of those precautions and ceremonies, he had been stolen away by the Sun and the Moon. So said the legends, fifty generations on. Half of the entire construction of Schooled wizardry had centred on that particular legend and all the ramifications—magical and political and cultural—wizards and politicians and canny or foolish emperors had built from it.)

You found the source of the rot.

Perhaps there had been a death here, an animal or a person. A moment caught into rottenness, the power generated by their passing tangled into a knot of corruption, a curse. It was hard to tell, now, whether the malice was intentional.

No matter. You need not judge, need not assign guilt or fault or innocence or penalty.

(You knew, I knew, we all knew that a catastrophe caused by innocent negligence or deliberate testing of safeguards was still a catastrophe; that even if the fault of the Fall was not mine, that I had not intended it, never worked to that end, never even imagined it a possibility; nevertheless I bore the guilt of many small decisions, and some that were not so small, that had permitted the fault-lines permeating Astandalas to grow so unstable.

And yet—would I, could I, dared I say that I would not still make those same decisions, even knowing this consequence?

And so: I could not but accept the penalty set before me, this crown I abhorred and this divinity so thoroughly undeserved, this life sentence given me for my crimes. There was a painful elegance to it, exquisite and agonizing as only the justice wrought by fate could be. In my most audacious years I would not have dared write a poem with such a savage symmetry to it.)

Your own magic roused, eager to act. You should need to enter a trance to be able to grasp this, but this morning the magic presented its plea before you and your magic surged forward in intuitive response.

You set your hand on the trunk of the tree before you. You relished the smooth texture of the bark, the silvery-grey colour, the waxy white-and-yellow flowers blooming in intermittent clusters on the bare limbs.

You thought they were scented, thought you knew the flowers from your baths, white and yellow, sometimes with their throats flushed with orange and pink, floating amongst the candles of an evening. You could not smell them now, not with the magical rot filling your nose.

Your hand on the tree. Your guards silent behind you. The Palace behind them, a hollowed, hurting beehive. The gardens caught between Zunidh and the destroyed Ysthar under Astandalas and the tangled and torn scraps of other worlds once knit into a careful whole by the wizards.

Never mind them and their hoards of salt, for an hour or a morning (or a year or a century) I would do what I could do by my own skills and knowledge.

One hand on the tree. The sun on your head, hot on your shaven crown.

(I had not been outdoors in the sunlight with my head shaven and uncovered, not since I was a … youth.)

Focus, you, I told myself, yourself, wishing I, you, had a name other than what was on everyone's lips but those addressing you. No matter that.

No matter that.

Hand on the tree. Sun on your head. Fresh air ruffling your clothes, brushing across the tops of your feet in little puffs of coolness. Magic knotted and tangled before you, a hundred spells once chained together now disjunct, dysfunctional, useless and worse than useless: destructive, twisted, broken.

Your own magic (*my own magic*), settled, eager to act, ready.

One distant bell rang the third quarter of the hour, sending little chiming echoes across the gardens, like the teal vase resonating with your footfalls.

You summoned your own power, the fire and brilliance at the heart of you, and silently, discreetly, serenely—oh, joyously, confidently, gleefully—worked.

By the time you had disentangled the magic in that one set of gardens it was past noon and you were irritated with the Ouranatha.

You returned to your aerie at the top of the Emperor's Tower, up the spiralling ramp for you would not show your unfitness by gasping for air, a fish out of its element, climbing up the seven flights of stairs.

The bells had rung the hours of the morning as you worked, each of them catching a piece of magic, a shred of order, and you had caught those flying scraps, trimmed their edges, gathered the unravelling threads, pieced them once more into a whole.

It was not the same whole it had been. You used no incantation or cantrip, no herbs or crushed stones or oils, no incense or purified water or smoke. No salt. No blood. No gold.

I spun magic out of the air, into the air, the wild magic in its garlands of bees and butterflies, petals and leaves, wind and sunlight and shadow and stone. The bells chimed, hours and quarters and the four great quarters of the day. I wove that in, too, those strictures and those structures, no longer kinked but coiled, no longer strained and stretched but folded, looped, knotted.

The magic rhymed across the space delineated by the bells: not symmetrical, not too tightly wrought, not too mannered; loose, leisurely, confident. It was not the words I had once written, not the music I had once composed, but it was something good and fine, these iterations and alliterations, this piece of magic consonant with that other, that assonant, this like a near-rhyme and that a visual pun and this other the deep underlying drumbeat of a metaphor.

All magic was metaphors, in the end.

(A conversation, once, very long ago:

The true art of poetry, I had declared, *is the art of giving names*.

And the person to whom I was speaking, carelessly, preoccupied with his own art: *I thought that was philosophy?*

My delighted response, an idea that would shape half my own sense of self: *Then perhaps philosophy is truly a branch of poetry. This pleases me.*

Some would say that poetry was a branch of magic, but I wondered. I wondered.)

I worked my way around the Palace, the bells spooling under my fingers, each toll an echo and an inspiration, a moment of joyous order in a chaotic mess. But fire was chaotic, and creation, and there were—not *rules*, not even laws, but—principles, yes, principles at work. All supposed rules of poetry could be broken, if you were good enough.

Magic was, I knew (I hoped, I prayed, I *wished*), the same.

I would not rebuild the Empire. I could not; and anyway, even if I had not worked towards its end, even if I had tried to redeem and reform the (*your*) corrupt court and government and army and priesthood rather than destroy it, nevertheless — oh, this was a shameful secret, for you who was not supposed to feel shame; you who was not supposed to do anything that might cause you to feel shame — I was *glad* it had fallen.

If only it could have happened without —

I would never be able to count the dead and destroyed. I could only accept the penalty fate gave you, bow my head before its yoke (you who bowed to no one), and do the work set before me to the best of my ability.

Point and counterpoint, thesis and antithesis and synthesis, none of it symmetrical, none of it *bound*. Even in a sonnet, a sestina, a couplet, a clerihew I had never obeyed all the rules.

When I finished I was light-headed with exhaustion and satisfaction, quite possibly sunburnt on the top of my head. I — *you* — paced slowly up the long, winding ramp, all seven flights up to the rooms at the top of the Emperor's Tower, past courtiers and servants and secretaries who regarded your process with uncertain awe on their faces, in those moments before they bowed, after they rose, in the corners of your eyes.

You read the report Cliopher had prepared for you that afternoon.

It was obviously Cliopher who had started to prepare the morning reports as well. This was the same neat hand, the same quick economy of phrase, the same limpid clarity of thought. Three pages for the report, summarizing an unwieldy mass of policy, propaganda, overt activity, covert operations, conjecture, and fact.

You read the report twice, a third time, thinking.

The policy: the Ouranatha acted as the mediator between the gods, including the Last Emperor, and the people, by their prayers and their magic holding the forces of chaos and disorder at bay.

The propaganda: that they had prevented the *complete* destruction of the world in the Fall, in the aftermath of the Fall; that they continued with their ancient prestige and power because they were the only ones able to convey the power descending upon the Lord Emperor and radiate it out to bless and provide succour to the people.

The overt activity: they had not only continued, but actually increased, many of their rituals, ceremonies, and holy-days, with the avowed intention of assisting the reconstruction after the fall.

The covert operations: there was a huge amount of bribery, blackmail, and other forms of corruption going on to hide the ineffectualness of their magic and to accomplish many of the same results. They were very cautious about what exactly was said in the reports passed up to you.

The Ouranatha had positioned themselves as the primary authority in the dark and bewildering days immediately after the Fall, with the previous lord magus, Lady Jivane, in full compliance. When *you* had awoken after the Fall, Lady Jivane had immediately handed over her authority to you. The Ouranatha had supported this, knowing you to be a reasonably effective ruler and no magic-user.

Most of the College of Wizards had been in the city itself during the Fall, and therefore had perished with the rest of Astandalas that was not contained within the Palace walls. Those elders remaining in the Palace, and their immediate apprentices and attendants, had declared themselves the inheritors of all the power of Astandalas, and had appointed to their number those they felt would fall in line with their purposes.

They had been concerned when it turned out you *could* do some magic, but so far all the public works had been sufficiently minor—calling light was the most dramatic— that this discovery had not changed their approach. They continued to establish themselves as the most significant authority, drawing in the best and brightest minds from the aristocracy and the army to swell their numbers, consolidating their position in the Palace and expanding outwards from there. They had been subordinate to the aristocracy and the army in late Astandalan days, a point which had always chafed the elders.

The conjecture: they intended to be a theocracy with *you* as their figurehead god and the nine elders the actual rulers.

The fact: their magic no longer worked.

You set aside the report, stacking it neatly on your desk. (Not *perfectly* neatly, though someone would undoubtedly straighten the irregular corners by the time I returned.) You went into the inner chambers, let the Cavalier an Vilius and your other attendants disrobe you, remove the jewels and gold with their gloved hands and their long dressing wands. The guards stood at attention, steady and precise.

In times past the Emperor's closest attendants had worn veils of translucent muslin, embroidered with sigils and secret runes, imbued with aromatic mixtures, to protect them against the eyes of the Emperor. The same cloth was used still for the gloves, in case of a clumsiness.

(They were very well trained. Not even the tip of a glove had touched me since that poor woman I had burned with my hand.)

You went into the baths: a steam room for sweating, a small pool for plunging into cool water, the great bath in which you swam of a morning. There were other rooms as well, some you used occasionally and some which had been required for the ceremonies attendant on the emperor and which you had gladly set aside.

Your grandmother, the Empress Anyoë the Short-Lived, had had the baths built in their present form. She had chosen the tiles: lions and peacocks, the blue-green of the tiles matching the vase you had found in the Treasury. (My woken magic whispered that they were from the same hand, the glaze from the same vein of copper threading through a mine in central Voonra.)

Your head was throbbing. You could not bear the steam room for long; you suffered the Cavalier to scrape your skin clean and trailed by guards, by servants, by attendants bearing towels and tweezers, unguents and oils and soaps, wash-cloths and pumice stones and long-handled clippers to trim the nails of your toes, you went into the tepidarium and lowered yourself into the cool, fresh water.

Anyoë's attendants had worn veils. She had had a consort, father of her children. He would have undergone the thousands of rituals over the hundreds of days required for intimacy, for sharing the great canopied bed.

(And her children? Had the midwives and wizards taken them from her before their eyes were opened? At what stage had the taboos come into effect? When they were nine, the age at which an aristocratic child of Astandalas was presented to the outside world? When they were weaned, if she had nursed them herself? When the umbilical cord was cut?)

You got out of the pool, water streaming down from your body, ignoring the water darkening the mosaic surround (ignoring the mosaic, those ancient serpents and lions, flowers and birds, those more recent cavorting satyrs and nymphs) except to be sure you did not slip and fall. The guards might try to catch you, after all, in human instinct.

You went to the large pool. There too you disregarded your guards, your servants, your attendants, even the mildly perplexed expression on the Cavalier's face for this deviation from your usual routine, and you swam.

Anyoë had rebuilt the baths. Her son, your uncle Eritanyr, had covered the rooms with pornography and extended and overextended the armies of Astandalas in a hunger nothing had ever satiated.

And then there was you, hundredth and last Emperor of Astandalas, who had been trying somewhat ineffectually to reform a corrupt government when the fault-lines slipped and you became forever and ineluctably written into history as the one reigning when the Empire of Five Worlds fell.

It was inexplicable that you had survived.

Your body was loose and languid when you finally emerged from the bath. At some point the sunset bell had tolled and your guards had changed. (The new ones were Tisua and Ser Ergaz, respectively the son of a merchant from Alinor and a minor Ystharian lord.) The Cavalier was still there, waiting with a soft cotton robe. It was no formal garment; it was a soft, cloudy lilac, like a distant island on a hazy day.

You put on the robe and let the Cavalier anoint you with a lotion; it was soothing on your head. You still felt odd. Despite all the increasingly obvious problems with the magic around you, you felt ... pleased.

You informed the Cavalier you would not go down to hold court that evening, the first words spoken since that morning's interaction with your secretary, and went into your private study for your usual hour of solitude.

The door closed behind you, closing the guards on the outer side.

The room had once been a storage room, and when you decided it would be *your* place it had already contained several items of ancient furniture long since removed from the main chambers. There was a divan in a style you were fairly certain went back half a dozen reigns. It was odd even for you to think that perhaps Zangora XIV herself had sat upon it, snuggled that dip into the cushions, worn that gently thinned patch of velvet. The divan was an odd colour, between puce and orange, and you occasionally wondered what other furnishings had been in those alabaster rooms for her to think it a good colour.

You sat down on the divan, hesitated a moment, swung your feet up, and then swung all the way around so your head was on the seat and your feet dangling over the arm-rests. The one high window, unscreened, showed a black square of the evening sky. You had not lit any lights coming in, and so as your eyes adjusted to the dim room the black square performed the visual trick of brightening into a fine clear ultramarine even as the night outside grew darker.

You let your head rest on the velvet, listening to your blood throb and your scalp tingle with sunburn. If your grandmother had had her baths and your uncle his pornography, surely you could have something other than a vase and a tapestry to make these rooms *yours*?

Your breathing slowed, steadied, and you found yourself falling into your magic, into the deeper trance, without conscious thought or effort.

I could not *see* magic, not directly. I felt it, heard it, tasted it, knew the shift of its texture and the scrape of it in my mind. When I entered the deep trance I could see it: my own and that without. I had tried it only once since the Fall, when I realized that my passive magic had come back to me, and nearly lost myself in the horror of the destruction.

This time I was prepared for that chaos, and held to my purpose. My actions that morning had created a cleared and safe place, somewhere I could stand. I stood there, for a moment, looking at the task that awaited me. The snarled magic was as impenetrable as the thorns around the sleeping princess in the old fairy tale.

(In that banned poem *Aurora*, the princess at the centre stole her own way free with the assistance of her hand-maiden, leaving the competing princes to throw themselves at the thorns. I had always thought it a better tale than the old legend. The castle besieged by magic was such a *small* part of the story.)

The metaphorical presentation of my own magic was as blasted and broken as everything else.

I had a certain affinity to fire, and once had imagined the heart of myself as a fire, something burning brightly in a forest glade, fresh and wild and free. Now I stood at the edge of an ashy waste, the old trees and shadowy guardians dim and far away in the fog.

The ashes were not all scattered and salted. There was, a little off-centre, a ring of smooth stones, gleaming golden-white, with a young flame burning within them. I stepped forward, barefoot here in my imagination, clothed in wine-red trews and purple tunic with silver buttons.

The stones holding my fire, protecting it from draughts, were pearls, fist-sized and irregular and yet gleaming, even glowing, golden with the reflected white flash of the fire. I touched one: the pearl was warm as the bath-water, warm as the sunlight on my head, warm as someone's hand in mine.

There was no wood nearby, and I nodded to myself, resigned, knowing there was still so much work to be done.

~

At midnight you summoned the Ouranatha, and the Ouranatha came.

Why it all had to happen within the compass of one day you did not know, but yet you knew it was so. You had emerged from the trance as the first hour of the evening sounded forth, your glance resting unseeing on the objects in your study as you lowered your feet and raised yourself upright. Your magic burned peaceably within you, a candle-flame in a glass tower; and you knew what you must do.

The nine elders rose when you entered the Swan Chamber, their robes heavy storm-grey, silver mantles above, carved silver and gold and copper masks over their faces. The room was lit by candles, for their magic was not reliable. You smiled faintly as you entered, ideas and their consequences falling into your mind one after the other, like lines in a poem or chords in a song.

So. So. Before the dawn of the new day you would change things.

It was time for you to take control, to be the Lord Magus of Zunidh, for you could not be the emperor and you would not be a god. And neither were what was needed, in this moment of this day. What was needed was not a mere figurehead and a squabbling priesthood, a threadbare bureaucracy, a decimated army, a warring aristocracy, an ineffectual wizardry, a battered populace.

You had one good guard who stood firm no matter the provocation, and one good secretary who had no sense of self-preservation, and you were yourself emperor, lord, priest, and mage. Neither Astandalas as it had been nor Zunidh as it currently was gave much heed to anyone outside of those categories. (At least, I told myself, neither

Cliopher Mdang and Ludvic Omo were aristocrats, nor even from the heartland. It would have to be enough.)

You had changed into half court costume in black and gold, your jewels black opals with a rolling flash of gold and orange and blue to hint that you met the elders primarily in your capacity as Lord Magus of Zunidh, whose colours were bronze and orange and blue. The Cavalier an Vilius had nearly smiled when you specifically asked for that costume to be brought.

The quarter bell tolled midnight as you stood in the doorway, surveying the room. Nine white-wood chairs; nine elders; one throne. Your two guards, who had been with you since halfway through your reign as Emperor (Hlinar of Norsamite on Colhélhé; Tuah of Vrigang also on Colhélhé), stood in their customary positions at the door. No one else was in the room.

You strode to your seat on the throne at the top of the room. Ebony inlaid with ivory and nacre from the shells that produced the golden pearls, elaborately carved and gilded lines. It had been in the Throne Room proper at one point, built to represent the bringing of the Wide Seas into the Empire. Ebony from Jilkano, ivory from the sea-elephants once found in the waters of the island of Nikian, the golden mother-of-pearl from those remote islands far, far across the Wide Seas.

(Why *had* Cliopher sayo Mdang come to the Palace? Had he been stranded on this side of that wall of storms by the Fall, or had he passed through it, following whatever strange and unlikely ambition had brought him here? For whatever reason he had come, he had begun scattering those pearls, small gifts cast almost unheeding, one hand catching *mine* and holding me fast.)

You regarded the Ouranatha for a long few minutes in silence, considering.

The priest-wizards' formal costume had not changed in colour or general effect in millennia, although even in your lifetime you recalled shifts in fashion for buttons and hood and cut. The heavy, bulky, formless robes of this iteration hid most of their bodies, muffling your ability to read their postures. The grey was the shade of a heavily overcast sky, pregnant with rain.

Your magic swirled around the room, tasting, testing theirs. One or two of the elders shifted uncomfortably, more sensitive to wild magic or less disciplined than the others. No matter. Their magic was as tangled and incomplete as that outside in the grounds and woven through the Palace, incantations and spells spoken and performed without response.

At length you steepled your hands together. You made no pretence at not looking at them. *They* were safe behind their bespelled masks, of course, even if the taboos had held.

There were times when all politics was about compromise, about balancing powers and principalities and thrones, about weighting every carefully chosen jewel and even more carefully chosen word. There were times when even the Emperor had to be careful lest he lose the support of those below him, and lose—well, not his throne; it was rare indeed for an Emperor of Astandalas to be actually *deposed*—but lose, yes, the actual power. If the bureaucracy sided with the army or the Ouranatha, the aristocracy lost.

But *you* had the bureaucracy, or at least Cliopher sayo Mdang, on your side, and there were not so many members of the Imperial Bureaucratic Service left that you did not know just how much power that one man would be able to wield, given the opportunity and the support.

And you had your core guard, the Imperial Guard, who stood by you. The old generals from your uncle's reign, who had regretted your lack of enthusiasm for their wars, were almost all of them dead and gone in the Fall, leaving behind those who willingly served *you*. Those who did not now belonged to the Ouranatha or the outlying aristocrats who had not yet come back to the Palace.

What did the Ouranatha have? All their current authority, by all their own words and gestures, by the belief of the populace and the actions of the government, descended from *you*. They had the semblance of power; you had the reality. As soon as they realized that, truly understood that, they would give first the appearance of complaisance and then the actuality. That was how power *worked*.

"After careful study of the situation," you said, your voice rolling through the silent room, "we have begun the active restoration and recreation of Zunidh's magic."

The elders shifted and mumbled, constrained by the ancient rules of etiquette but their surprise obvious. You regarded them with your face serene, noting that the rules of etiquette did in fact hold; that an even more ancient rule of human behaviour was in effect.

Give lip-service to an idea long enough and it would take hold.

No matter that none of these men and women *believed* you a god, any form of divinity: they spent the majority of their days carefully, deliberately, actively inculcating that belief in those around them. They had worked *desperately* to ensure that you were considered a living god, centre of the world, hope in the darkness after the Fall. Your position there gave them their position here.

You moved your gaze around the room. This afternoon, thinking about Anyoë, thinking about the sunlight on your head, thinking about your poor thin thread of a fire, you had imagined confronting them about those rituals and ceremonies and taboos. For a moment you had thought you would make a grand personal declaration denying their existence, defying the hundreds of years of custom.

But this was not the moment. *My* personal, internal views were irrelevant here. This was the moment in which you took up the power you were given by rote prayer.

Any moment now the elders would break free from their surprise and break the customary observance of subservience. You must not let them take control, not let them know they *could*.

Even with one guard and one secretary beside you, you were only one man, and all your knowledge but for the magic you had wrought that day was mediated by men and women such as these.

So. So.

You looked around the room, serene mask meeting copper, silver, gold.

Every great mage learned early to furl his power, hide it behind layers of apparent ordinariness. Even without the taboos there was magic in your eyes when you let it rise, magic in your hands and your skin, in your voice and in your blood.

It had been so long since you had done this. There had only been a few times even when you were young that you let your magic expand fully, wings opening, the fire roaring free of the constraints.

It was easy, so easy.

You—*I*—let the magic rise, filling the room, calling to Zunidh who had claimed me, whom I had claimed. The Palace magic responded, the bells chiming here in this room, echoes of their actual sounds. The candles streamed and blew out with a thought, my undifferentiated magic illuminating the room, a rolling flash of power that crashed against the walls of the room and expanded out into the halls, through the whole half-asleep shell of the

Palace, out across the gardens where I had walked that day—

And then Zunidh caught me, some part of the world grasping hold of the hand I held out, my magic arcing out through all the tangled and snarled masses, in one bright surge skipping lightly out, a sunburst reflected mirror to mirror in a flash from lighthouse to ship lost at sea.

I held it there for a moment before I let the wave subside, the light dim, the magic recede and fall back, tired and ready to nestle into my heart and wait for the next call.

The Ouranatha sat there in still, shocked silence.

The quarter-hour bells did not ring between midnight and dawn, but I knew their rhythms; I knew that for all that had been a singular moment, and an infinite one, it had also occupied a mere quarter-hour of the day.

(There were not many magi who could expand their magic enough to fill a full quarter of an hour of time.)

I furled the magic back, sure it gilded my eyes as gold as the state portrait, my skin as luminous as ever it had been with the magic of Astandalas.

But this was *my* magic, my choice, my doing.

Into the stunned, surmising silence you said: "We thank you for the work the Ouranatha has been doing to maintain the spirits and morale of the populace, and to bind as best you could the magic broken in the Fall. We expect that as we continue to settle the and restore the magic your own spells will come once more to be properly ... effectual."

Another silence, the Ouranatha indistinct figures in their heavy storm-grey robes, their silver hoods, their metal masks. You did not let the lights dim entirely, left the room glowing softly, golden-white like early dawn.

You listened to the tenor of the room. Waited. The elders looked at each other, one by one. There had long been a rumour that the masks let them speak mind-to-mind with one another, one of the reasons for their great effectiveness in debate.

One of the elders, the one wearing a mask of gold, the High Priest of the Sun (*your* high priest, according to their own stories), raised their hand in the traditional request to speak.

You inclined your head in agreement.

"Glorious One," the elder said in a rich alto voice, "we are most grateful and overjoyed to hear you say it. We are eager to assist you in the great and difficult work before you."

You did not smile, in triumph or amusement. You inclined your head again, letting the magic glimmer and glitter around you. "We are glad to hear it," you said simply, and then, for you had not been sure, not *quite*, that you retained enough authority for this to work: "We thank you for your attendance upon us this untoward hour."

And with that you rose and accepted their accustomed obeisances, so practiced and smooth and devoid of meaning (and yet, for all that, wearing the habit of thinking of you a certain way into their minds), and strode back to your own rooms and your own bed.

When, the next morning, you bade Cliopher request the Ouranatha to release their hoards of salt to the usage of the people, Cliopher forbore comment; and the elders provided what you requested, with only a single, meaningful comment praising you for your benevolence to *all* your people, great and small.

THE LITTLERIDGE TREATY

There were no ill effects to your spending the morning outside in the sunlight, unless one counted your sunburned head. This the Cavalier an Vilius certainly did: he demonstrated more emotion than he had any previous occasion, humming and clicking and making distressed noises in the back of his throat, when he noticed the skin peeling the next day.

You didn't mind all that much. It was an unusually sharp sensation, unpleasant certainly but not exactly unwelcome. The lotion the Cavalier rubbed in was cool and soothing, and you found yourself asking for a container of it to take into your private study.

You had forgotten you might have your own creams, apply them to your skin yourself. It was hardly necessary to be private, though somehow it felt much more intimate to rub the cream into your own head than to sit there while your attendants used their gloves and their sponges and their other tools to do so for you.

You massaged the lotion into your scalp before working the remainder into your fingers. You kneaded your hands together, staring at your own skin glistening with the cream, in the faint light coming in from the one high window. Gulls were crying not far outside, circling the tower.

Your nails, manicured and buffed smooth and gleaming. The dark skin above, the paler skin on your palms, the creases forming the lines palm-readers used. You traced out the lines with your thumbs, first your left hand and then your right. The cream smelled of calendula and chamomile, northern herbs far from the usual array of your perfumes.

Divination had never been one of your skills, though you had sometimes been able to scry, and very rarely had fleeting glimpses of other places and other times. Sometimes you later walked into those fragments, a moment unexpectedly doused with familiarity.

The bell rang three-quarters and you sighed and closed the lid on the lotion container. It was a fine enamelled dish, the cork lid fitting snugly inside the lip. You weighed it in your hand, taking in the pretty depiction of tiny figures in a bucolic scene: farmers in wide hats, sheep, a weeping willow. The container came from Voonra; the lotion primarily Zunidh with a few additions out of the stores from other parts of the Empire.

That snarl of magic outside the Palace, and yet *you* still had cosmetic lotions containing oils and flower petals from the far side of other worlds.

You set the dish on the top of a pile of books. The pile overbalanced and scattered volumes and loose papers across half the room. You almost left it alone before you remembered that your most successful rebellion against the customs hedging you had been the repulsion of all of your staff from this room. No one else was going to pick up the books if you did not.

You did not object to the mess, really, but some part of you rebelled at the idea of leaving the books crumpled and in such disarray. You bent over and picked them up, realizing as you did so that it was quite literally years since you had last *picked up* fallen items.

The books were mostly histories you'd read in the middle part of your reign as emperor, when you were trying to find some parallels for a complex situation in western Colhélhé. Two hefty legal tomes had been precariously balanced in the middle of the stack. You flipped through them, wondering why they were in here. Legal tomes belonged in the small library on the other side of your public study, where you could refer to them in the course of drafting laws and judgments.

They both had to do with the Collian situation. You glanced through the text of one, remembering long nights of studying the texts, sifting through precedents and the judgements of past emperors. You still had them half-memorized, once your memory was jarred by seeing them.

You looked around the room, suddenly critical. This was supposed to be your retreat, your refuge, your one place where you did not have to be The Emperor, and you had brought in legal tomes and histories? You looked at the papers crumpled in your hand. Notes on the dispute, notes on the countries and peoples and tribes and individuals involved — notes on Colhélhé and its place in the Empire —

— A scrap of poetry.

You realized you were panting, and stopped deliberately. Three breaths in, three breaths out. (My face and body were calm; I had to remind myself I could relax my posture, and I had not.) Attempts at two lines of poetry, the concluding couplet of a sonnet I had never finished.

I read over the lines blankly, stupidly, unable to process the words.

I knew when I had written them, or at least the approximate date. Sometime in the middle few years of my reign, seven or eight years in, when I no longer expected much to change, I had found it within me to write poetry once again. I had been coming into my own as a ruler, more confident in my understanding of law and custom, more able to look at myself in the mirror and see the Emperor of Astandalas.

In this room I had never been The Emperor.

I sat down again on the divan and spread the paper out on my knee, pressing out the creases as best I could.

~~In the heart~~
~~In the centre~~
~~In the hearth~~

Start again, I remembered admonishing myself.

~~In the cell~~
~~In the prison~~
~~In the oubliette~~

My hands were trembling. I pressed them into my knees, the fleshy muscle above the bone, through cloth that slipped under dry fingers.

My own slanting letters, a scrawling slash through all the unsatisfactory words. The ink from the nib spattering a fine black mist across the paper. I rubbed my thumb against where the pen callus on my finger ought to be more prominent. I no longer had all the other calluses I'd once worn proudly, physical reminders of things I had once done, a person I had once been.

Your first grooms of the chamber had spent hours with lotions and pumice stones, rubbing them out.

You had let them, for what could you do? As emperor there had not been time to play the standing harp, the lap harp, the ardrin, the lute. You had barely been able to write.

There had been no magic and no music for you, nothing you could create. There had been all the magic of the Empire spinning around you, all the music of the court. You had tried, had instituted prizes for new music, had

patronized musicians and magicians and masters of a
hundred arts, hoping to help others if you could not help
yourself.

(It had not helped, except to show me what I looked
like to those who looked upon me, safe at their seven ells'
distance: the glowing, gleaming, golden figure high on the
throne.)

I had, in what was then my half-hour of solitude in this
room, slowly extracted poetry from myself. Seven years
before I had come to the point of being able to write a
hundred sonnets, except that I had never finished the
last one.

I was (you were) the hundredth emperor of Astandalas.
Somehow completing the hundredth sonnet of that
sequence had seemed as if it would ... bind you. If I never
finished the sequence, some part of me had reasoned at a
level far, far below reason, perhaps I would never quite
finish becoming The Emperor.

I had written the poems, never reading them over once I
had written them, not until I had come to the hundredth
and last and hesitated there.

A day turned into a week, and a week into a month, and
a month into a year, and you buried yourself in the Collian
legal tangle and the question of the contested southeastern
border of Astandalas on Alinor and all the thousand other
problems for which you were supposed to supply the
solution.

A year turned into another, and another, and one day
you realized you had not picked up your pen—that you had
not *thought* to pick up your pen—for nearly a second seven
years.

Seven years to become an apprentice, and seven years
to become a master, said the crafter guilds of Kavanor
before they all fell into the sea. Seven years to become

something of an Emperor; seven years starting to become a good one.

It was the week before the winter festival of Silverheart began, the fourteenth year of your reign. You had listened to the songs proposed for the yearly prize, recognizing one particular composer from the previous years. Their songs were … fresh, joyous, beautiful (of course), but there was something so light about them, so purely happy, that you had struggled with your serenity, with the aching desire to *yourself* create in answering joy.

You had come, I had come, into your study, found the piles of law-books and histories, and the novels and narratives that teetered in other stack arounds the room, and you had found that sheaf of sonnets.

Reading them for the first time since I had written them, I had been struck over and over again by the realization that I had *forgotten* —

I had been so angry at those poems, which played on stone and shadow, light and air, prison and freedom, the body and the soul and the heart that could not be bound, but could — oh, how it *could* — bind itself —

So angry that I had forgotten I was imprisoned. So angry that I had been reminded I was free.

So angry at my own skill as a poet, and so angry that I could not *be* a poet — for if it were known that *I* (that *you*) had written those poems, the whole edifice of your authority might have come crashing down with the doubts and the fears and the stubborn refusal to *stay where I was put* —

I had decided I would publish them to the winds, since I could not publish them openly. I climbed up onto the table and onto the chair upon the table, reached out that one unscreened window, and threw the sheaf of poems into the air, to be taken by the winter slush and snow, the wind, the unknown.

I had regretted it all of three minutes later, of course, but by then it was too late.

In the heart
　　In the centre
　　In the hearth
　　In the prison
　　In the cell
　　In the oubliette
　　Seven years ten months nineteen days five hours one crown

I had stopped there, one savage scrawl that was no part of any sonnet, and the bells had rung, and *you* had gone out to prepare for whatever you had been doing next, for whatever it was did not matter: not even a week after that you had been sitting in the small library, reading over a book on the fiduciary responsibilities of the Grandees of Southern Voonra, when the world crumbled out from under you.

The bells rang.

You went out. You closed the door behind you, the only one you ever touched, and looked at the long tapestry, the eastern wall with its fading luminosity as the day wore on.

Something shifted inside (the kaleidoscope clicking shut?), and when the Cavalier arrived with your lunch you told him to draw up plans to add a terrace to the Imperial Apartments.

The new pattern: you performed your morning routine. You read Cliopher Mdang's neat reports over breakfast, meditated on your magic, considered the state of the world, and then you met your secretary for the morning's greeting and the following work.

Each day you went through the workings of the government, the decisions you had to make and the information you needed to have. Cliopher would then take the decisions and proclamations and notes and disappear to whatever he did the rest of the day—to disseminate your decisions and then write up the reports for the next morning, presumably —while you went outside to continue your slow progress attending to the magic around the Palace and grounds.

While you were outside the crafters came to create the terrace whose design you had approved. They could not work while *you* were present, of course.

(I was so grateful for that excuse to leave the Apartments. It helped to have the excuse, though not even the Ouranatha came to tell me—*you*—not to push the customs too far. They did not need to.)

You descended to the Treasury and to the Imperial Archives, toured the offices of the bureaucrats (discovering Cliopher sayo Mdang at a desk there, once, surrounded by piles of reports and apparently happy), toured the barracks of the Guard, met with aristocrats, met with the Ouranatha, met with those who had taken upon themselves the work of government, bestowed benedictions on your people.

The magic was tedious and slow work, difficult and finicky. You were not accustomed to such painstaking work, and had to stop often to remind yourself there was no expectation that you could do one grand and glorious gesture and have it all back to what it was.

You did not *want* it to go back to what it was, and surely
—*surely*—you were not the only wild mage—the only *person*
—who felt so. The aristocrats and the priest-wizards and
the army and even the bureaucracy had liked the previous
system, but your people?

(Oh god, my poor people.)

The more magic you worked, the more at home you
felt with the new world. You touched every piece of
Astandalan wizardry, binding them into your new
working, learning to keep it accessible to those who
had studied the cantrips and the spells, the stones and
oils and blood and smoke and salt. You wove magic
into magic, and with each pass around the Palace in
the spiral outward, more and more of the city settled
down.

Cliopher sayo Mdang slowly began to ask permission to
take on other responsibilities, hire other staff to assist him.
You agreed to most of the requests, amused that your secretary seemed determined to position himself as the man
behind the throne. He was intelligent, intrepid, competent,
unpolished, and funny: there were far worse people to have
standing there.

Time spooled on, still snarled and strange, but less so
with each passing day and concomitant work of magic.

And each day the opening in the wall to the new terrace
took further shape.

～

The more you stabilized the magic, the more disordered the
aristocrats seemed to be.

It was all very well, you thought as you read through
report upon report of war and squabbles and threats of war,
for the surviving aristocracy to decide to consolidate their

power and muster armies in order to create and maintain order after the Fall.

It was understandable that, as the weather and the magic (very slowly) started to become in better order, they would want to continue to consolidate their power and authority, and not incidentally expand their reach.

It was, in your opinion, entirely wrong for them to take the excuse to oppress their populaces and start laying waste to crops and industry.

(Oh *god*. When had I become so cynical? All these numbers and names, black ink on white paper, stark and simple. I was not supposed to know what a war was like, what it *meant* to have crops laid waste and houses razed to the ground. I was not supposed to be able to feel the sweat and the blood and the flies. I was not supposed to be able to imagine the stench of charcoal and burned flesh. I was not supposed to be able to picture the ruins and the hollow-eyed survivors. I was not supposed to be able to *know* that exhaustion and that flat, flattened heart —)

The fourth time you received word that the saltworks in the town of Littleridge had been destroyed — this time by the forces under the so-named King of Tlaxos, who was in constant warfare with your own great-aunt, the Princess Anastasiya (who had, somehow, survived the Fall and was now running the former Marquisate of Exiputal with an iron fist and a surprisingly effective navy), the still-calling-himself-a Duke of Zborowanda, even though Zborowanda itself had fallen with Kavanor, and —

Black letters on white paper. Each name a report on a high aristocrat of the court, people you knew or had known, people to whom you might even be related. As if all that mattered was the number of ships in Princess Anastasiya's navy, or swords under the banner of the King of Tlaxos; as if the people who crewed those ships, held those swords, were nothing and less than nothing.

As if you did not know that the salt from those salt-works meant that the great tuna run up through the Dagger Islands of the Alixerian Sea would not be preserved, and that therefore there would not be enough food through the coming lean season.

As if you did not know that each time Littleridge was sacked a dozen or a hundred soldiers lost their lives, and a hundred or a thousand civilians had their lives broken and scattered for all that their heart and lungs might still work to keep them alive.

As if you did not know that each drop of blood spilled, each hope fractured, each dying or grieving moment, did not catch the magic of the place and tangle and snarl it into the sort of curses a war wreaked on the generations ahead of them. Each savage cut a scar on the land, on the people, on the future.

The Commander in Chief of the Imperial Guard, who had been one of the most powerful courtiers in your imperial court (and whom I had respected, if never quite liked), called it *a mess*.

A mess.

Each time a report came from the archipelagos and peninsulas of the Alixerian Sea between the continents of northeastern Dair and western Kavanduru there seemed to be another petty ruler and their increasingly complex alliances in the mix.

Nearly the entire eastern hemisphere of Zunidh was now embroiled in *the mess*, or perilously close to being so. Only far northwestern Mgunai, Jilkano, and, of course, the islands of the Wide Seas were still aloof, and that was almost certainly due solely to lack of proximity.

This was not about salt, or food, or sea-rights. This was

about power, and authority, and status: the blood that had filled the Treasury with gold, broken into fragments along the fault-lines that had already slipped when Astandalas fell.

You sat there with the reports, the new magical order humming close, comforting. *Here* there was order, the widening circle of order around the Palace. How far out had you reached? Not even to the Solamen Fens you could see out the alabaster-traced window, with their baleful spirits and their monsters. Not even to the Grey Mountains to the west, or the necropolis of your ancestral dead to the north. Barely past the river to the south.

You sat at your desk. Only the guards were there, this afternoon when you were supposed to be working magic. You should be out of the room so the terrace-builders could continue with their work.

(It seemed such an obscenely unimportant thing, that terrace, when the world was like this. And yet it helped to see the mess and the broken wall and know that the crafters would turn it all into something good. If only it were not *I* who was responsible for all the broken world.)

The sandalwood desk. The cool air, hints of lemon and vanilla this morning. Your signet ring on your finger; you were worrying it with your thumb, and made yourself stop.

There was so much to do.

You wished you might just slump and bury your head in your hands, but that was a child's wish. There was no one else to do this, no one else who *could* do the magic, and as for *the mess* in the Alixerian Sea ...

You let yourself sigh, eyes on your painted self, serene features and flat gold eyes and all the visual trappings of power, and then you turned back to the reports in front of you. Somewhere in here there would be a thread, a clue, a way forward.

Somewhere.

It became clear that someone needed to go to Littleridge.

You considered the available people.

There was yourself. On the one hand, you had the power and the responsibility, and probably also the authority; on the other, it would be an insane amount of work to merely get yourself there. Not to mention there might be serious repercussions from a magical perspective if you left the Palace and in its central positioning within the new order you were building.

(There was no way, not with the world in the state it was, for me *not* to be the centre. The spider spun her web out of her own being; she could not leave it and still spin the filaments into order.)

There was the Princess Indrogan, your effective prime minister. She was the logical choice to send, perhaps, but she was …

Well, she was better suited for jobs that did not involve cautious and careful negotiation. Princess Indrogan tended to believe in brusque direction as the most effective form of leadership, and you knew enough of enough of the people involved in *the mess* to know that they would not respond well to her style. Princess Anastasiya barely accepted *you* as her superior; she would never listen to an upstart princess from a lesser house.

There was the Commander in Chief of the Imperial Guard, but he tended to look at every war as an exercise in military prowess, and it was a fact that you had no army loyal to you beyond the actual guards in the Palace.

There was the Ouranatha, but a major reason for not permitting them to become a theocracy was that they were not good at governing even themselves. The number of schisms and internecine squabbles the priest-wizards got into was a lesson in what to avoid.

The aristocrats were the problem.

The people had nothing but the few leaders already muscling into the mess. The Shark Queen of Dinezi had her own concerns to deal with.

The problem was that you could think of no one besides yourself whom all the parties would even *listen* to.

The next morning, you greeted your secretary and returned to your pacing, silent at first. You stared at the portion of the tapestry map representing the eastern hemisphere of Zunidh. Littleridge was near the Dagger Islands, right at the narrows of the Alixerian Sea between the Eastern and Northern Oceans.

In the old days of the Empire there had been a major naval base there and a trading city of some hundred thousand inhabitants, which had kept order in the region. Both city and navy had been destroyed in a volcanic eruption during the Fall, and it was said that the region now was one of the most fractured and fragmented with respect to time. The King of Tlaxos was twenty generations on from the Fall in his little kingdom; Princess Anastisiya had barely two years to work through the grief of losing almost all she knew.

You paced.

Up to the jewelled nightingale, twenty-five down, ten back to your desk. If you left the Palace —

But how?

(And did you really think, did I really think, that I could *actually* soothe all those warring aristocrats and would-be kings and shape peace? How did I know I would not be entirely overcome by the magic there? Even from here I could feel the sullen throbbing knot, magic and human emotion feeding into each other, spiralling ever deeper into chaos and woe. Closer to hand — ?)

Fifteen paces up, twenty-five down, ten back to your desk. You were so *tired*.

Going to an active war zone would not be a holiday.

It was still somehow tempting —

Something exploded.

You staggered, catching yourself on his desk. Your head was ringing, your eyes filled with whirling sparkles. You gripped the desk hard, the silky surface for once hard under your fingers, your nails gouging into the wood. Sandalwood filled the air, incongruously strong, like temple incense.

One breath, two, three. There was no noise in your ears, no cries or crashes.

The eruption was —

Far away. You let out another exhale, breathed in deeply, straightened, looked around.

Both Cliopher and your guards had stepped forward, hands wide and hovering, faces concerned but the taboos still holding.

You carefully peeled your hands away from the desk, even as you tried to gather your scattered thoughts. Somewhere far to the north there had been an eruption that had punched through the magic of the world, jerked your careful weaving askew, tugged the ground from beneath your feet. But you were here, you were alive, you were upright.

This was going to do something awful to the situation in the Alixerian Sea. For a moment you could only just keep yourself from laughing aloud at the terrible absurdity of the situation, the interconnections that while broken and tangled were still there—oh god, I couldn't leave, I couldn't face the sea journey—so contrary to my magic!—from one barely-there moment of order into the chaos of a war zone while the whole polar region poured disordered magic across the north of the world as if it were the aurora borealis—

Cliopher stepped forward. "My lord? Is there anything I can do to assist?"

You were too tired to suppress your first sarcastic reply. "I don't suppose you want to go knock some sense into those idiots at Littleridge, do you?"

Silence. Dead, incredulous silence.

When was the last time I used the informal singular out loud?

The magic was throbbing, as if I lay upside-down on my couch, staring at the floor above me, all the blood rushing to my head. My guards and my secretary stood there, staring, shocked as the Ouranatha when I let all my magic unfurl.

I laid my hand on the sandalwood table, for something to touch. The room was spinning, the kaleidoscope turning, the magic swarming, the lights flickering, faltering—

"If my lord desires it, I shall go gladly."

—I stopped.

Deep breath in, deep breath out. My hand on the table. The cool air on my head. The perfume in my nose, lemon and just a hint of warm amber, something else bright-green like a growing thing. Cliopher Mdang looking steadily at me, his brown eyes sharp and seemingly aware of what he was offering.

—*Someone* had to go.

Into the war zone, into the chaos, into the battling would-be nations. Cliopher sayo Mdang was not a soldier or an aristocrat or a priest or a wizard. He was a Fifth Degree Secretary of the Imperial Bureaucratic Service. No one would think he was setting himself up in authority over them.

(Would anyone actually listen to him?)

He was an exceptionally talented secretary. Even if all he did was organize them *slightly*, get them to talk to one another, that would be —

Even a few *days* of an actual ceasefire would be a help.

I could not go, not with whatever had just happened in the Northern Ocean. I was not sure I would be able to cross the room without stumbling, the way I felt at the moment. I took several more deep breaths, trying to compose myself, trying to think.

"There has been a magical ... disruption," you said by way of vague explanation, gesturing in a direction that was almost certainly not the right one. "I shall ... We shall be occupied with it for ... a while. It will require our full attention."

You winced as a sharp retort reverberated down the continent-spanning lines of magic. Whatever was going on was huge and potentially disastrous. You could not go to the north, not with the world as it was.

(Even in Astandalan days how *could* I have gotten there quickly? Flying horses only existed in certain stories. They were not here, not now, not even for you.)

I would have to descend into the deepest trance and hope my scrying skills were up to the needful.

"Very well, my lord," Cliopher said, as if you had given him full and explicit directions. He started to gather his materials together. Before he was quite finished he looked up at you, concern in his eyes; but it almost seemed as if the concern was for *you*, not the situation. "Is there anything particular you hope I can accomplish on your behalf?"

"Oh, peace," you said, your tongue unruly, sarcastic, savage. You gripped the smooth edge of the sandalwood desk with your hand. Your voice flattened out with exhaustion, which almost sounded like serenity. (Almost.) "Peace."

"Very good, my lord," said Cliopher Mdang, as if that were a perfectly reasonable thing to ask of him, and he made his obeisances and left.

You spent an indeterminable period of time sitting at your desk with your hands around a cup of tea, staring at the steam eddying and swirling in the room.

Inside your mind the fire of your magic was burning high, still off-centre and still surrounded by the ashy wasteland, but the mist was not so thick, and the fire burned brightly. I spent little time with it, turning my attention *out*.

(I could not wonder about that hearth of irregular pearls, golden as the tithe-offerings from the islands of the Wide Seas. I had still not actually asked Cliopher where he was from, why he had come, who he was.)

The relationship between natural processes and magical ones was always much more complicated than it seemed at first. Some theorists held that magic *was* a natural process, as much a part of the larger whole as the weather; others that it belonged to a higher or a lower order of reality, hence its ability to work on both the physical and the intangible, even unto the soul.

You thought—well, I had many thoughts on it. I fancied, sometimes, that my youthful ideas were correct, and both poetry and magic were about naming things truly. Knowing the true name of a thing was a very, very old magic indeed.

(But poetry, I was nearly sure, was older. Primary. Words first; then magic.)

If you were to be a great lord magus—and I thought it

surely would be easier than being a great emperor, for I was not philosophically and morally opposed to the fundamental existence of the lords magi—you would have both the opportunity and the need to think deeply about such things.

In the moment, you could only say that magic affected nature, and nature affected magic, and human activity affected both.

In the far northernmost reaches of the continent, there had been in Astandalan days a polar ice cap. Ocean currents in the Northern Ocean had been constrained by the great Xiputl peninsula to the west and the mess of islands and promontories of northwestern Kavanduru, bounded in the narrows of the Alixerian Sea even now being granted the quiet, unpolished competence of Cliopher sayo Mdang.

(I had asked no practical, logistical details. The reports came; somehow people travelled, with armies if not for trade.)

The western half of Kavanduru extended north and east before being cut by the bays of the Damaran side of the continent, while on the other side of the ocean, Northern Dair ended in the great nearly-inland Boreal Sea embraced on its other side by Mgunai, which reached out another peninsula, almost a subcontinent, of its own.

The Fall had set off a series of volcanic activity through much of central Northern Dair. The entire agricultural heartland had been destroyed by lava flows, and a chain of volcanoes leading north into the Boreal Ocean had melted much of the polar ice.

This had then flooded the northern side of Mgunai, causing a group of weather-witches to attempt to fix the problem on their own, but their particular combination of Astandalan wizardry and homegrown witchcraft was unstable at the best of times. They had been in the midst of an elaborate ritual—the echoes of it tangled with everything you could feel coming out of the the north—when yet another volcano had erupted.

Human magic met natural magic and set off a cascade of events that had, so far as you could tell, ended up with the complete destruction of the polar ice cap, the flooding of the former Ikikaks tundra, and some sort of effect on the world's magnetic field.

Well.

It wasn't *that* different from taking a mess of any description and cleaning it up, really.

Not that this was something you enjoyed at all. I rather preferred *making* the mess, to be truthful. But there was no one else to do this work, and so ... you did it.

You resolutely did not think of the people. You couldn't, not at the moment. No matter how much you missed—*I* missed—

Keep working.

$$\sim$$

You lost track of the hours and days.

You could not spend forever in the trance, could not work magic at that level of distance and difficulty and detail all the hours of the day, and so every once in a while you would surface to the physical world and attend to your bodily needs.

(How I missed the morning routine. Ludvic was on the night rotation now, and none of the other guards would meet my eyes.)

You had told your attendants and guards to see that no one disturbed you except for direst emergency, and so your ambit shrank to the well-worn path between bedchamber and baths and official study. You did not go into your private study, not with your mind buzzing and half-soused with magic.

The awful thing was that it was exciting.

I had never worked magic like this, so complex and so grand in scale. I found it ... enjoyable. It was hard, but hard in a way I had forgotten things could be: every moment I was learning something new about magic, my magic and the magic of Zunidh and magic in general, and I was also working to the good of the world and his people, and ... it was fun.

(You must not think of the people on the other side of this magic. You *cannot* let yourself be mired in the details. You must hold to the through-line, the end resolution, make every detail fall into place within the overall, each a syllable in a poem, each a note in a song; each a note in a *symphony*. You could not let yourself ask the question of who was behind that note, that syllable, that flicker of magic. *You must not.*)

I plunged deep into the magic, sleeping with my mind still touching the lines of power, the explosive force of the volcanoes, the fiery edges of the tectonic plates scraping against each other, the green masses of the forests growing up where there had once been permafrost. The rest of the world's climate shifted warmer with the melting of the ice, returning to what ancient legends said had been the case long before the Empire was more than a fledgeling kingdom.

How long did it take?

(How long was it taking those negotiations in the Alix-erian Sea? The knots were still tight and tangled, the magic sulky and recalcitrant, deforming the grand sweeps in the arctic as the currents through the narrows between Xiputl and the Enamboloyan peninsula bore the polluted magic with the northbound waters.)

In my sleep I dreamed of centuries unfolding, the forests growing, the fields expanding, people starting to move in, taking up the healed and healing magic and weaving it into their own little works and needs.

I woke and wrought anchors and guided channels, taking up the desires for lights and warmth and good fortune, protection against wild animals and monsters and bad weather, the need for fertility and the lingering echoes of the Wild.

(You were not the only one to dream of the Wild. The calling, crying song was there, faint in the distance as a breath of snow from high mountains; but there. Unlike the wizards of Astandalas *you* cared for it, for those who heard that song, that call, and you left a space for it, for them, for you, for me.)

Some length of time into this there was a sudden easing of the tension, as a rope snapping.

I held the mass of magic in my mind, my hands still around the cup of tea, my feet on the floor and my posture excellent even as my soul, my heart, seemed to rock backwards under the sudden release.

A deep breath, another, another. Remember Ludvic standing rocklike at the corner of your bier, letting nothing rock him. Hold on to his steadiness, his steadfastness, his strong shoulder.

I tugged tentatively at a metaphorical line, edge of a tangle of magic, and—it slithered untangled, so I sat there (in your cool, alabaster study, sandalwood and jasmine in your nose, lambent sunlight in your eyes, pouring in through the half-build door, the traceried windows, the air like fresh water in your mouth), with the magic all puddled around me like robes that had slipped off my shoulders.

I touched the magic, fearful of what had happened, and —it settled.

It was as unexpected a benison as that morning my own magic had settled.

I could not tell if it would hold, how long this reprieve, this ceasefire, this moment would last. Human emotion roused magic, as magic roused human emotions, so a curse or a blessing, a conflict or a cornucopia, fed back and forth between imagination and action, nature and soul.

There was a moment of respite, and after my first, shocked surprise, I hastened to take advantage of it.

I had once been good at improvisation. It had been so long—

I gathered up the magic in my hands, the fabric of the land in silken folds. I worked quickly, not slapdash but in great impressions, the grand gestures I had once loved so dearly. *Here* a knot tied to the top of a turning mountain peak (how? Why? No time now to ask why that peak spun slowly, ponderously, whimsical as a giant first learning the concept of humour); *there* a line channelled through a river gorge, threading the needles of stone bridges and caverns; *here* a set of stitches, an embroidery sampler on the landscape, of the landscape, magic emerging from and returning to the stone, air, water, fire—

The waters rushing through the Narrows of the Alixerian Sea, the aurora borealis spinning beauty out of the solar wind (and was your ancestor the Sun watching to see what you did?), the forests spearing up out of the former tundra, the stars scattering down largesse like rain—

The volcanic fires settling, subsiding, fire in the earth, warmth under my feet, under my hands. Lifeblood of a continent, geysering forth, steam and slow rivers of lava winding their ways down to the new seas, cooling, hardening, mimicked by the glaciers that calved next to the pebbled beaches where the seals and walruses lay.

The air full of clouds, of mist, rain and snow, generous;

the sun a great glory for half the year, then resting in starlit shadow, letting the land rest and the thin skin of life turn inwards to quiet creativity.

Oh hold, *hold*, I prayed the ceasefire, as my hands took up the notes of the symphony, directing, conducting the magic along the line I had chosen—

The guard at the door thumped down his spear.

I blinked, starry-eyed and muzzy-minded from the magic, and after a moment let the power sift through my fingers, sand falling down through the pinch of an hourglass. I had told my guards not to interrupt me except in case of dire emergency. I could not ignore them when they judged it one.

Ludvic was on guard once more, with a new partner as Sergei was coming close to retirement.

(And if it had been centuries in northernmost Dair, where those lands had grown forests, those mountains glaciers, those volcanoes islands, what had it been here?)

I was in my study, seated at my desk, the ever-present cup of tea still steaming hot before me.

"Well?" I said, mustering my strength for this new disaster. Not all of them were magical, and thus something I would have noticed.

"Cliopher sayo Mdang has returned, my lord," said Ludvic.

Internally I held still. So. So. He had survived the journey out, the war zone, the squabbling aristocrats, the journey home.

He had done *something* to ease the tension.

—Could it possibly be—I dared not hope for *good news*—but—

I gestured for Ludvic to open the door.

And.

And.

Enter Cliopher sayo Mdang. He was still in his grey-brown Fifth Degree Secretary robes, and there was something worn and travel-stained about him. Had he not thought to change his garments before coming to report?

"Good morning, Sayo Mdang," I said, and something clicked into its proper place as he rose from his obeisance and returned the greeting.

"Good morning, my lord."

And he met my eyes. He did. (Oh gods above, *he did*.)

Cliopher's eyes were sly and laughing, even if his face was more or less composed and professional.

(He must, I thought fleetingly, drive his fellow secretaries to distraction, with his demeanour so reasonable and his eyes betraying his constant amusement at their antics. Had he managed to keep his eyes down, dealing with the princes and lords and petty kinglets at Littleridge? He did not manage before the Lord Emperor despite the taboos, so … probably not. The thought gave me inordinate pleasure.)

Then I realized—*his eyes were laughing*.

This could not possibly be good news, could it?

(That tension had eased, the knot coming undone. I had laid out all the lines of magic, pinned and knotted them into a new order, knitting fractured parts into a new whole.)

"You have a report, we take it?"

I made my voice, your voice, retain its usual neutral intonation.

(I had barely spoken all the time he was gone. My mind full of magic, but still. Still.)

"Indeed, my lord." Cliopher had learned the gestures, and at my brief hand movement put himself into a more ready and easeful posture. He was holding his leather writing box and now opened it to extract a rolled sheaf of papers. After silently requesting permission he set this on the table before standing back expectantly.

I considered the man: Cliopher's eager bearing, his bright eyes, his attempt to hold his face neutral, and the thickness of the papers thus presented to me.

He was a magnificently *competent* secretary, but even so. Even so.

I said slowly, "Be so good as to summarize your activities in Littleridge, Sayo Mdang."

Sayo Mdang tilted his head slightly to one side, like a dog or a bird considering the item before them. Then he said, with a very fine attempt at nonchalance, "After researching the situation and meeting with all the parties, I was able to guide them to a sufficiently satisfactory outcome, namely the delineation of regional borders as provinces under your Radiancy's rule."

—What the hell?

I picked up the tea cup and took a sip, trying to make sense of what he'd just said.

Surely Cliopher Mdang had not gone off to broker a ceasefire between independent warlords and would-be kings and come back with a peace treaty establishing a new world government?

"Sufficiently satisfactory?" I eventually managed, for want of any better response.

"Inasmuch as even those participants who would have preferred a higher final rank will, I believe, hold to their accord, should you be so willing as to confirm it."

What the *hell*.

"We shall have to review the articles of the agreement," I said, not exactly as cautiously as I ought.

"Indeed, my lord," Cliopher Mdang replied demurely, with a bright, satisfied light in his eyes.

~

It *was* the outline of a new world government.

I read through the treaty draft with an entirely unaccustomed feeling of awe. *I* was supposed to be the great governor, the mediator, the judge: and yet I did not think, had I gone to Littleridge, that I would have come up with this.

(Of course I would not have come up with this. *I* did not want to be an emperor or king; but it was not fair to all those who prayed to you as a god to let the world continue to devolve into violent chaos as various men and women fought for power and control when I, or rather my secretary, could do something about it.)

The first part of the treaty was a preamble discussing a vision for the future of the world. It was a future of peace and prosperity, of stable government and reclaimed culture and trade.

(I had not thought, *you* had not thought, of the future, any future, beyond what the present unspooled towards.)

I traced out the vision Cliopher had described, created out of his own mind, his own culture—oh, I wanted to know more, I could *see* he was drawing from some source I did not know, some perspective on the world so different and yet so beautiful, he was so quietly *sure* of where he came from, where he was going—and—oh.

Oh.

Cliopher had not only spoken to each of the leaders, from Princess Anastasiya Yra, daughter and sister and aunt and great-aunt of emperors, down through to the delegation sent by, yes, the Shark Queen of Dinezi. He had spoken also to their soldiers and sailors, their officers and their cooks, their servants and their doxies and their suppliers, and to all the people he could find who still lived in the contested town of Littleridge and its neighbouring islands.

All of them were here; all of their voices were here.

I read over the report again, taking note now of the

laconic references, the footnotes referring to some history or law. What a *mind*.

(What a gift he had come here, to the Palace, to turn that mind to the government of the world. How *close* I had come to losing that.

Blindness would not have stopped that mind, forestalled that brilliance, but breaking that taboo? In imperial days he would have been executed for the temerity. And what a *waste* that would have been. What a wasteland the world might have stayed. What a wreck *you* would have remained, a slowly desiccating remnant of a man.)

His approach was one I would never have thought of.

Cliopher Mdang had persuaded the warring factions to tell him their understanding of the source of authority, and since they were all still children of the Empire, their authority came theoretically from *you* down through their titles and holdings.

"There are," Cliopher explained when I questioned him on the details several days later, "several parties who greatly desire to be granted titles by you to establish their legitimacy."

I regarded my secretary thoughtfully.

(I must promote him. Cliopher deserved to wear the colours proper to the Emperor's personal secretary, at the very least. The red and black would suit him much better than the grey-brown of the Fifth Degree. What title could I grant *him*? What could possibly be appropriate?)

We were back in my official study, Cliopher at his desk and me once more pacing. I was standing just now not far from the teal vase, which glowed like the sea at dawn in the morning light. The new terrace was finished, and a clear glass doorway flooded light into the room in a shifting oblong.

(Sometimes a rhombus, sometimes a trapezoid, sometimes a mere quadrilateral, depending on the time of day and the angle of the sun.)

Almost all the up-room length of my pacing, ten strides to my desk, fifteen to the nightingale, I could see outside, across the new limestone terrace with the shade canopy, and then out over the floodplains of the river as it meandered to the sea. The sun was a great golden ball in the burnished sky, the blazing sea.

"You disagree?" I said, wondering at Cliopher's tone when he spoke of parties desiring to be titled.

Cliopher hesitated a moment, but at my encouraging gesture started to speak. He began calmly enough, his accent its usual slightly-softened twang, but as he continued to speak his voice gained in liveliness and his accent sharpened to a knife-edge.

"The structure of the Astandalan government was fundamentally tyrannical," he stated, without a blush or further hesitation. "The Emperor held his authority under the principle that he descended by blood and magic and right directly from the Sun, and being thus of divine blood had also divine authority. He granted titles and holdings to those below him, and thus permitted them to partake of that divine authority, theoretically according to what was mete and deserved. Those who did not have titles, it was understood, were not seen as being worthy of such by the Emperor, and thus were *actually* lesser than those who were."

I wanted to say any number of things in response to that, but bit my tongue. I did not disagree with either the account or Cliopher's obvious disapproval of the theory; but then again, a full hundred emperors of Astandalas had managed to maintain their rule and even their dynasty based on this principle, so those who upheld it were not *utter* fools.

"Even in those areas where it appears it has been substantially longer since the Fall than we in the Palace have experienced, this theory of authority has continued to exert its force. Thus those warlords and similar who are not *known* aristocrats of the Astandalan hierarchy sought and are seeking legitimacy by marriage and acknowledgment."

Cliopher paused there.

I tried for a neutral statement. "There needs to be *some* source of authority, do you not think?"

"Of course," Cliopher replied, "but it comes from the people, not the gods. Granting titles to those smart and skilled and strong enough to be good leaders only reinforces the old hierarchy and tyrannical systems of the past."

I stared at my secretary, who seemed to have forgotten entirely to whom he was declaring this wholly treasonous conception of political authority.

I glanced once at Ludvic, who seemed to be fighting to maintain a straight face, and then continued to pace, more slowly now, as I listened to Cliopher Mdang expound fulsomely on his theory of government.

Outside the new terrace door the gulls were wheeling. A flock of macaws rose up out of the trees in the gardens below my tower, long red and blue tails streaming behind them.

If I were not going to ennoble my secretary for his work at Littleridge, I mused—and from Cliopher's passionate description of how there surely could be a more equitable distribution of authority if one could only teach *everyone* they had a voice and a place and power of their own, he clearly would not be pleased by an aristocratic title—then what could I do to show my appreciation?

I listened carefully, but Cliopher never gave any suggestion of an honour he thought appropriate to someone who agreed with him.

I didn't know enough—I didn't know *anything*, really, except for what I had gleaned from Cliopher's approach in the sheaves of reports he had so far presented to me—about the cultures of the Wide Seas. I knew nothing more than where the Vángavaye-ve was to be found on the map, and that the illustration in the *Atlas of Imperial Peoples* suggested that the amused, reflective glint in Cliopher Mdang's eye was not entirely limited to himself.

But that did not help me come up with a culturally appropriate gift.

(I still wasn't entirely certain where Cliopher Mdang was from, come to think of it.)

Once I was finished with the situation in northernmost Dair, or as finished as I was going to be for now, I spent some number of hours in the small library, searching accounts of earlier emperors and their households.

I took the books outside, to sit on my new terrace with the air warm on my skin but shaded by a canopy of heavily embroidered cloth, red figured with gold because I had finally told the Cavalier I wanted something other than black and white and yellow.

(The Cavalier had startled and then said, *of course, glorious one*, and brought swatches of cloth for me to consider, dozens of fabrics in scores of colours, an abundance of choice.)

Whether it was the fresh air or the sunlight or the ever-improving magic or the tentatively establishing peace, so the reports were no longer *only* of disaster after disaster, war and pestilence and famine and storm, I felt ... better. More whole. More alive.

I took great pleasure devising titles for the warlords and

unwarlike leaders of the new provinces and underlying demesnes, and attempted not to crib too much from certain banned epics. I helped smooth out a few boundaries, judged a few conflicts, worked a few great acts of magic to improve the marginal lands that otherwise might have erupted again. I read about the evolving courts and households of my ancestors as the magic of Astandalas grew in complexity and might.

It was only in the past twelve or fifteen generations that the taboos had grown as stringent as I had found them. Each kingdom that fell to the armies of Astandalas had had to be bound into the whole, and each of those bindings had been anchored in the person of the Emperor.

Before the full height of this development the person of The Emperor had been sacred, but there had been no *actual* effects to touching. Zangora IX, who had had seven consorts and a dozen concubines (the historical record was somewhat coy as to whether these had been sequential or not), had not had to have them all undergo the rituals and ceremonies Zangora XIII's three consorts had.

Long ago, I discovered, when the taboo against touching started to come into full, terrible force, there had been a position called *the hands of the emperor*.

It had previously been something of a title for the head of the army under Zangora X and XI; the army had been greatly powerful in those days, showered with titles and tithes. The position transitioned by easy steps to an office in the court. Zangora XIV had made her consort her Hands; she had been one of those not exactly deposed, but whose authority had eroded by foolish decisions, until that one good choice. It had been so brilliant of effect that the next eleven emperors had all appointed someone to be their *hands*, until Tyr IV had had some sort of falling out with his and switched to a body of councillors instead.

I had never found much to appreciate in the body of councillors I'd inherited from my uncle. They had expected my cousin Shallyr to become Emperor and had hoped I would be as much of a puppet ruler as they had anticipated him likely to be.

Those particular councillors had not lasted long in their positions, once I was able to think about my role and what it truly meant.

But in those days I had not had the time nor the energy to go researching alternatives beyond what I could myself come up with, and had merely appointed other people to the same positions.

There had, anyway, been no individual I dared *trust*. Not all my court had been incompetent, but they had all been seemingly corrupt. I sometimes thought my uncle had delighted in encouraging the rot, a kind of game of solitaire he played with himself.

(I played games of courtly solitaire as well, as one must when stuck high on a resplendent throne while everyone else danced. I had had an elaborate scoring system for both the literal dancing and the game of courts my courtiers played.)

What might I have done, with a trusted person at my right hand?

The Hands of the Emperor was as flexible an office as the Emperor needed it to be. Like physical hands, able for many tasks, big and small, grand and petty, holy and mundane.

The literal hands for those ceremonies that required the Emperor to touch; the means by which his divine authority was passed down to those below him.

I smiled at the thought, crossing the threshold of the door to the terrace, going *outside*. My guards stood at the door, in the shade, as I left them behind and ducked under the canopy to my seat. The sky was silvery blue washed with pink, no clouds on the eastern horizon but a few small ones, low down, blazing a hot, rich, molten gold.

The Hands of the Emperor. It had a good ring to it.

It was a way, perhaps, to touch the world neither as its tyrant nor as its god, but as a man doing my best to listen, to learn, to be. I could not eject myself from my place at the centre, not as the world stood now, not when I was still, always, the *believed* source of authority and power, and the actual lord magus working to restore that part of the world.

Perhaps *restore* was not the right word.

Cliopher Mdang's vision of what the future could be was not a *restoration*. It was a reformation; even a revolution. Something new built out of the pieces of the old, fault-lines and fractures mended with care, some invisible, and some brushed luminous as polished pearls with gold.

(In my inner landscape the fire burned steadily brighter; outside the ring of golden pearls the blackened earth was starting to sprout a fine green fuzz, and the mist was no longer quite so clammy, so cold. In the outer landscape, in the inner world, there was still so much work to be done. And yet … the fire *did* burn, no longer burned out.)

And so. And so: a title for Cliopher Mdang that did not, quite, imply that only a noble could be of worth in this new world you, *we*, were building out of the ashes of the old.

I watched the macaws flying, their red tails pennants in the sun, the river winding through green fields to the sea. The palace behind me, below me, embracing me; but the world before me, its scents in my nose, its sounds in my ears, its airs on my skin.

The dawn bell rang, and the sun rose in my eyes, dousing the land in light, catching the pale thatched roofs of village huts on the plain like pebbles, like pearls, like earth-bound stars. The macaws cried out in harsh voices, screams echoing through the lambent air, all too unmusical, all too real.

I closed my eyes and leaned back in my chair, the sun on my face, for a moment slouching, for a moment merely ... myself.

(And if I were humming *Aurora* quietly to myself, there was, for this one, shining moment, no one else to hear.)

Printed in Great Britain
by Amazon

21786814R00067